I0654243

MARI WOLF
RESURRECTED

The Complete Short Stories of Mari Wolf

By Mari Wolf
Edited by Greg Fowlkes

Includes the Special Bonus Story
AND NOW A MESSAGE...
By Greg Fowlkes

MARI WOLF RESURRECTED

The Complete Short Stories of Mari Wolf

© 2011 Resurrected Press
www.ResurrectedPress.com

All rights reserved. No part of this book may be used or reproduced in any manner without written permission except for brief quotations for review purposes.

Published by Intrepid Ink, LLC

Intrepid Ink, LLC provides full publishing services to authors of fiction and non-fiction books, eBooks and websites. From editing to formatting, to publishing, to marketing, Intrepid Ink gets your creative works into the hands of the people who want to read them.
Find out more at www.IntrepidInk.com.

ISBN 13: 978-1-935774-95-2

Printed in the United States of America

OTHER RESURRECTED PRESS
SCIENCE FICTION

Philip K Dick Resurrected:
The Complete Works of Philip K Dick

James H. Schmitz Resurrected:
Selected Stories of James H. Schmitz

H. B. Fyfe Resurrected:
The Works of Horace Brown Fyfe

Murray Leinster Resurrected:
Science Fiction Stories from the 1950's

Alan E. Nourse Resurrected:
The Works of Alan E. Nourse

Edmond Hamilton Resurrected:
Classic Stories of Edmond Hamilton

Evelyn E. Smith Resurrected:
Selected Stories of Evelyn E. Smith

Robert Sheckley Resurrected:
The Early Works of Robert Sheckley

Stanley Weinbaum Resurrected:
The Complete Short Stories of Stanley Weinbaum

And more!
Visit ResurrectedPress.com
to see our entire catalogue!

FOREWORD

The usual sources, Wikipedia and the Internet Speculative Fiction Database, offer little in the way of biographical data on Mari Wolf. She was born August 27, 1927. She wrote a column called "Fandora's Box" for the magazine *Imagination* from the April 1951 issue until April of 1956 at which time it was taken over by Robert Bloch. She wrote a number of short stories in the early 50's, seven according to the ISFDB, and one novel, *The Golden Frame* that was published in 1961.

Her name does crop up in the reminiscences of various people about the West Coast fan scene at the time, usually in the form of "Mari Wolf introduced me to X at convention Y". She seems to have been well known and liked by both fellow fans and authors. She is described as an attractive young woman in her twenties, a fact that is born out by a photo of her from the period. Other details are pretty sketchy at best. Before she was married she lived with her parents in Laguna Beach, CA. She was married for a time to fellow fan columnist and author Roger Phillips Graham whom she met at a science fiction convention. Apparently the marriage only lasted a few years. There is a comment about her working as a wind tunnel designer, and a reference to her appearing in an article on amateur rocketry in *Look* magazine. The information paints a tantalizing but fragmentary portrait of an attractive, intelligent woman in her twenties.

What does remain is her work, the seven stories that have been collected in this volume. There is also a novel published in 1961, *The Golden Frame* of which I know nothing beyond the fact of its existence. While other works may exist, I have been unable to find any evidence of them.

The stories, themselves, are well written and deal with the typical topics of science fiction from the period, aliens planning to invade Earth, Martian colonists, time traveling spaceships, rebellious robots, but treated with a gentler touch than was usual at the time. There is a sentimentality to "The Statue" and "The First Day of Spring" that would do Bradbury proud, while "Robots of the World!", "The House on the Vacant Lot", and "The Very Secret Agent" show a sense of humor. The other two stories collected here, "An Empty Bottle" and "Homo Inferior" are more philosophical in nature, pondering respectively the origin of life and the results of the next step in human evolution. All in all, they are not a bad body of work to be remembered by.

As good a writer as she was, and with the contacts that she had made through her fan activities, it's surprising that there isn't a larger body of work, but, for whatever reason, she doesn't appear to have published a short story after 1954. Perhaps she became involved in other pursuits. In any case, Resurrected Press offers these examples of her work for your consideration.

Greg Fowlkes
Editor-In-Chief
Resurrected Press
www.ResurrectedPress.com

Table Of Contents

An Empty Bottle

Originally Published in *If Worlds of Science Fiction*, September 1952

An Empty Bottle

Hugh McCann took the last of the photographic plates out of the developer and laid them on the table beside the others. Then he picked up the old star charts—Volume 1, Number 1—maps of space from various planetary systems within a hundred light years of Sol. He looked around the observation room at the others.

"We might as well start checking."

The men and women around the table nodded. None of them said anything. Even the muffled conversation from the corridor beyond the observation room ceased as the people stopped to listen.

McCann set the charts down and opened them at the first sheet—the composite map of the stars as seen from Earth. "Don't be too disappointed if we're wrong," he said.

Amos Carhill's fists clenched. He leaned across the table. "You still don't believe we're near Sol, do you? You're getting senile, Hugh! You know the mathematics of our position as well as anybody."

"I know the math," Hugh said quietly. "But remember, a lot of our basics have already proved themselves false this trip. We can't be sure of anything. Besides, I think I'd remember this planet we're on if we'd ever been here before. We visited every planetary system within a hundred light years of Sol the first year."

Carhill laughed. "What's there to remember about this hunk of rock? Tiny, airless, mountainless—the most monotonous piece of matter we've landed on in years."

Hugh shrugged and turned to the next chart. The others clustered around him, checking, comparing the chart with the photographic plates of their position, finding nothing familiar in the star pattern.

"I still think we would have remembered this planet," Hugh said. "Just because it *is* so monotonous. After all, what have we been looking for, all these years? Life. Other worlds with living forms, other types of evolution, types adapted to different environments. This particular planet is less capable of supporting life than our own Moon."

Martha Carhill looked up from the charts. Her face was as tense and strained as her husband's, and the lines about her mouth deeply etched. "We've got to be near Earth. We've just got to. We've got to find people again." Her voice broke. "We've been looking for so long—"

Hugh McCann sighed. The worry that had been growing in him ever since they first left the rim of the galaxy and turned homeward deepened into a nagging fear. He didn't know why he was afraid. He too hoped that they were near Earth. He almost believed that they would soon be home. But the others, their reactions—He shook his head.

They no longer merely hoped. With them, especially with the older, ones, it was faith, a blind, unreasoning, fanatic faith that their journey was almost over and they would be on Earth again and pick up the lives they had left behind fifty-three years before.

"Look," Amos Carhill said. "Here are our reference points. Here's Andromeda Galaxy, and the dark nebula, and the arch of our own Milky Way." He pointed to the places he had named on the plates. "Now we can check some of these high magnitude reference stars with the charts."

Hugh let him take the charts and go through them, checking, rejecting. Carhill was probably right. He'd find Sol soon enough.

It had been too long for one shipful of people to follow a quest, especially a hopeless one. For fifty-three years they had scouted the galaxy, looking for other worlds with life forms. A check on diverging evolutions, they had called it—uncounted thousands of suns without planets, bypassed. Thousands of planetary systems, explored, or merely looked at and rejected. Heavy, cold worlds with methane atmospheres and lifeless rocks without atmospheres and even earth-sized, earth-type planets, with oceans and oxygen and warmth. But no life. No life anywhere.

That was one of the basics they had lost, years ago— their belief that life would arise on any planet capable of supporting it.

"We could take a spectrographic analysis of some of those high magnitude stars," Carhill said. Then abruptly he straightened, eyes alight, his hand on the last chart. "We don't need it after all. Look! There's Sirius, and here it is on the plates. That means Alpha Centauri must be-"

He paused. He frowned and ran his hand over the plate to where the first magnitude star was photographed. "It must be. Alpha Centauri. It has to be!"

"Except that it's over five degrees out of position." Hugh looked at the plate, and then at the chart, and then back at the plate again. And then he knew what it was that he had feared subconsciously all along.

"You're right, Amos," he said slowly. "There's Alpha Centauri—about twenty light years away. And there's Sirius, and Arcturus and Betelgeuse and all the others." He pointed them out, one by one, in their unfamiliar locations on the plates. "But they're all out of position, in reference to each other."

*   *   *   *   *

He stopped. The others stared back at him, not saying anything. Little by little the faith began to drain out of their eyes.

"What does it mean?" Martha Carhill's voice was only a whisper.

"It means that we discarded one basic too many," Hugh McCann said. "Relativity. The theory that our subjective time, here on the ship, would differ from objective time outside."

"No," Amos Carhill said slowly. "No, it's a mistake. That's all. We haven't gone into the future. We can't have. It isn't possible that more time has elapsed outside the ship than—"

"Why not?" Hugh said softly. "Why not millions of years? We've exceeded the speed of light, many times."

"Which disproves that space-time theory in itself!" Carhill shouted.

"Does it?" Hugh said. "Or does it just mean we never really understood space-time at all?" He didn't wait for them to answer. He pointed at the small, far from brilliant, star that lay beyond Alpha Centauri on the plates. "That's probably Sol. If it is, we can find out the truth soon enough."

He looked at their faces and wondered what their reactions would be, if the truth was what he feared.

*   *   *   *   *

The ship throbbed softly, pulsating in the typical vibrations of low speed drive. In the forward viewscreens the star grew larger. The people didn't look at it very often. They moved about the corridors of the ship, much as they usually moved, but quietly. They seemed to be trying to ignore the star.

"You can't be sure, Hugh." Nora McCann laid her hand on her husband's arm.

"No, of course I can't be sure."

The door from their quarters into the corridor was open. Several more people came in—young people who had been born on the ship. They were talking and laughing.

"Would it be so hard on the young ones, Hugh? They've never seen the Earth. They're used to finding nothing but lifeless worlds everywhere."

One of the young boys in the hall looked up at the corridor viewscreen and pointed at the star and then shrugged. The others turned away, not saying anything, and after a minute they left and the boy followed them.

"There's your answer," Hugh McCann said dully. "Earth's a symbol to them. It's home. It's the place where there are millions more like us. Sometimes I think it's the only thing that has kept us sane all these years—the knowledge that there is a world full of people, somewhere, that we're not alone."

Her hand found his and he gripped it, almost absently, and then he looked up at their own small viewscreen. The star was much bigger now. It was already a definite circle of yellow light.

A yellow G-type sun, like a thousand others they had approached and orbited around and left behind them. A yellow sun that could have been anywhere in the galaxy.

"Hugh," she said after a moment, "do you really believe that thousands of years have gone by, outside?"

"I don't know what to believe. I only know what the plates show."

"That may not even be Sol, up ahead," she said doubtfully. "We may be in some other part of space altogether, and that's why the charts are different."

"Perhaps. But either way we're lost. Lost in space or in time or in both. What does it matter?"

"If we're just lost in space it's not so—so irrevocable. We could still find our way back to Earth, maybe."

He didn't answer. He looked up at the screen and the circle of light and his lips tightened. Whatever the truth was, they didn't have long to wait. They'd be within gravitational range in less than an hour.

He wondered why he was reacting so differently from the others. He was just as afraid as they were. He knew that. But he wasn't fighting the thought that perhaps they had really traveled out of their own time. He wondered what it was that made him different from the other old ones, the ones like Carhill who refused even to face the possibility, who insisted on clinging to their illusions in the face of the photographic evidence.

$$* \quad * \quad * \quad * \quad *$$

He didn't think that he was a pessimist. And yet, after only three years of their trip, after only fifty Earthlike but lifeless worlds, he had been the first to consider the possibility that life was unique to Earth and that their old theories concerning its spontaneous emergence from a favorable environment might be wrong.

Only Nora had agreed with him then. Only Nora could face this possibility with him now. The two of them were very much alike in their outlooks. They were both pragmatists.

But this time there would be no long years during which the others could slowly shift their opinions, slowly relinquish their old beliefs and turn to new ones. The yellow sun was too large and urgent in the screen.

"Hugh!"

He turned to the door and saw Amos Carhill standing there, bracing himself against the corridor wall. There was no color at all in Carhill's face.

"Come on up to the control room with me, Hugh. We're going to start decelerating any minute now."

Hugh frowned. He would prefer to stay and watch their approach on the screen, with Nora at his side. He had no duties in the control room. He was too old to have any part in the actual handling of the ship. Amos was old, too. But they would be there, all the old ones, looking through the high powered screens for the first clear glimpse of the third planet from the sun.

"All right, Amos." Hugh got up and started for the door.

"I'll wait here for you, Hugh," Nora said.

He smiled at her and then followed Carhill out into the crowded corridor. No one spoke to them. Most of the people they passed were neither talking, nor paying any attention to anything except the corridor screens, which they could no longer ignore. The few who were talking spoke about Earth and how wonderful it would be to get home again.

"You're wrong, Hugh," Amos said suddenly.

"I hope I am."

The crowd thinned out as they passed into the forward bulkheads. The only men they saw now were the few young ones on duty. Except for their set, anxious faces they might have been handling any routine landing in any routine system.

The ship quivered for just a second as it shifted over into deceleration. There was an instant of vertigo and then it was gone and the ship's gravity felt as normal as ever. Hugh didn't even break stride at the shift.

He followed Carhill to the control room doorway and pushed his way in, taking a place among the others who already clustered about the great forward screen. The pilot ignored them and worked his controls. The screen cleared as the ship's deceleration increased. The pilot didn't look at it. He was a young man. He had never seen the Earth.

"Look!" Amos Carhill cried triumphantly.

The screen focused. The selector swung away from the yellow sun and swept its orbits. The dots that were planets came into focus and out again. Hugh McCann didn't even need to count them, nor to calculate their distance from the sun. He knew the system too well to have any trouble recognizing it.

The sun was Sol. The third planet was the double dot of Earth and moon. He realized suddenly that he had more than half expected to see an empty orbit.

"It's the Earth all right," Carhill said. "We're home!"

They were all staring at the double dot, where the selector focused sharply now. Hugh McCann alone looked past it, at the background of stars that were strewn in totally unfamiliar patterns across the sky. He sighed.

"Look beyond the system," he said.

They looked. For a long time they stared, none of them speaking, and then they turned to Hugh, many of them accusingly, as if he himself had rearranged the stars.

"How long have we been gone?" Carhill's voice broke.

Hugh shook his head. The star patterns were too unfamiliar for even a guess. There was no way of knowing, yet, how long their fifty-three years had really been.

*   *   *   *   *

Carhill shook his head, slowly. He turned back to the screen and stared at the still featureless dot that was the Earth. "We can't be the only ones left," he said.

No one answered him. They were still stunned. They couldn't even accept, yet, the strange constellations on the screen.

End of the voyage. Fifty-three years of searching for worlds with life. And now Earth, under an unfamiliar sky, and quite possibly no life at all, anywhere, except on the ship.

"We might as well land," McCann said.

The ship curved away from the night side of the Earth and crossed again into the day. They were near enough so that the planetary features stood out sharply now, even through the dense clouds that rose off the oceans. But although the continental land masses and the islands were clearly defined, they were as unrecognizable as the star constellations had been.

"That must be North America," Amos Carhill said dully. "It's smaller than the continent on the night side...."

"It might be anywhere," Hugh McCann said. "We can't tell. The oceans look bigger too. There's less land surface."

He stared down at the topography thousands of miles below them. Mountains rose jaggedly. There were great plains, and crevasses, and a rocky, lifeless look everywhere. No soil. No erosion, except from the wind and the rains.

"There's no chlorophyll in the spectrum," Haines said. "It seems to rule out even plant life."

"I don't understand." Martha Carhill turned away from the screen. "Everything's so different. But the moon looked just exactly like it always did."

"That's because it has no atmosphere," Hugh said. "So there's no erosion. And no oceans to sweep in over the land. But I imagine that if we explored it we'd find changes. New craters. Maybe even new mountains by now."

"How long has it been?" Carhill whispered. "And even if it's been millions of years, what happened? Why aren't there any plants? Won't we find anything?"

"Maybe there was an atomic war," the pilot said.

"Maybe." Carhill had thought of that too. Probably all of them had. "Or maybe the sun novaed."

No one answered him. The concept of a nova and then of its dying down, until now the sun was just as it had been when they left, was too much.

"The sun looks hotter," Carhill added.

The ship dropped lower, its preliminary circle of the planet completed. It settled in for a landing, just as it had done thousands of times before. And the world below could have been any of a thousand others.

They dropped quickly, braking through the atmosphere, riding it down. The topography came up to meet them and the general features blurred, leaving details standing out sharply, increasing in sharpness as if the valleys and mountains below were tiny microscopic crystals under a rapidly increasing magnification.

The pilot picked their landing place without difficulty. It was a typical choice, a spot on the broad shelving plain at the edge of the ocean. The type of base from which all tests on a planet could be run quickly, and a report written up, and the files of another world closed and tagged with a number and entered in one of the great storage encyclopedias.

Even to Hugh there was an air of unreality about the landing, as if this planet wasn't really Earth at all, despite its orbit around the sun, despite its familiar moon. It looked too much like too many others.

The actual landing was over quickly. The ship quivered, jarred slightly, and then was still, resting on the gravelled plain that had obviously once been part of the ocean bed. The ocean itself lay only a few hundred yards away.

Hugh McCann looked out through the viewscreen, turned to direct vision now. He stared at the waves swelling against the shore and his sense of unreality deepened. Even though this was what he had more than half expected, he couldn't quite accept it, yet.

"We might as well go out and look around," he said.

"Air pressure, Earth-norm." Haines began checking off the control panel by rote. "Composition: oxygen, nitrogen, water vapor—"

"There's certainly nothing out there that could hurt us," Martha Carhill snapped. "What could there be?"

"We might check for radioactivity," Hugh said quietly.

She turned and stared at him. Her mouth opened and then snapped shut again.

"No," Haines said. "There's no radioactivity either. Everything's clear. We won't need space suits."

He pressed the button that opened the inner locks.

*   *   *   *   *

Carhill glanced over at him and then switched on the communicator, and the noises from the rest of the ship flooded into the control room. Everywhere people were milling about. Snatches of talk drifted in, caught up in the background as various duty officers, reported clearance on the landing. Most of the background voices were young, talking too loudly and with too much forced cheerfulness about what lay outside the ship.

Hugh sighed, as aware of all the people as if he were out in the corridors with them. It was the space-born ones who were doing most of the talking. The children, the young people, the people no longer young but still born since the voyage started, still looking upon Earth more as a wonderful legend than as their own place of origin.

The old ones, those who had left the Earth in their own youth, had the least of all to say. They knew what was missing outside. The younger ones couldn't really know. Even the best of the books and the pictures and the three dimensional movies can give only a superficial idea of what a living world is like.

"Hugh." Carhill clutched his arm.

"Yes, Amos."

"There must be people, somewhere. There have to be. Our race can't be dead."

Hugh McCann looked past him, out at the sky and the clouds of water vapor that swirled up to obscure the sun. The stars, of course, were completely hidden in the daylight.

"If there are any others, Amos, we can be pretty certain they're not on Earth."

"They may have left. They may have gone somewhere else."

"No!" Martha Carhill's face twisted and then went rigid. "There's no one anywhere. There can't be. It's been too long. You saw the stars, Amos—the stars—all wrong, every one of them!"

Her hands came up to her face and she started to cry. Amos crossed over to her and put his arms around her.

Hugh McCann watched them for a moment and then he turned and left them and went out through the locks after the young people. He didn't know what to think. He wished that they had never turned back to Earth at all, that they had kept going, circling around the rim of the galaxy forever.

He went through the outer lock and then down the ramp to the ground.

He stood on the Earth again, for the first time since his early youth. And it was not the same. There was bare rock under his feet and bare rock all around him, gravel and boulders and even fine grained sand. But no dust. No dirt. No trace of anything organic or even ever touched by anything organic.

He had walked too many worlds like this. Too many bare gray worlds with bare gray oceans and clouds of vapor swirling up into the warm air. Too many worlds where there was wind and sound and surf; where there should have been life, but wasn't.

This was just another of those worlds. This wasn't Earth. This was just a lifeless memory of the Earth he had known and loved. For fifty-three years they had clung to the thought of home, of people waiting for them, welcoming them back someday. Fifty-three years, and for how many of those ship-years had Earth lain lifeless like this?

He looked up at the sky and at all the stars that he couldn't see and he cursed them all and cursed time itself and then, bitterly, his own fatuous stupidity.

The people came out of the ship and walked about on the graveled plain, alone or in small groups. They had stopped talking. They seemed too numbed by what they had found to even think, for a while.

Shock, Hugh McCann thought grimly. First hysteria and tears and loud unbelief, and now shock. Anything could come next.

*   *   *   *   *

He stood with the warm wind blowing in his face and watched the people. In the bitter mood that gripped him he was amused by their reactions. Some of them walked around aimlessly, but most, those who were active in the various departments, soon started about the routine business of running tests on planetary conditions. They seemed to work without thinking, by force of habit, their faces dazed and uncaring.

Conditioning, Hugh thought. Starting their reports. The reports that they know perfectly well no one will ever read.

He wandered over to where several of the young men were sending up an atmosphere balloon and jotting down the atmospheric constituents as recorded by the instruments.

"How's it going?" he said.

"Earth-norm. Naturally—" The young man flushed.

"Temperature's up though. Ninety-three. And a seventy-seven percent humidity."

He left them and walked down across the rocks to the ocean's edge. Two young girls were down there before him, sampling the water, running both chemical and biological probing tests.

"Hello, Mr. McCann," the taller girl said dully. "Want our report?"

"Found anything?" He knew already that there was nothing to find. If there were life the instruments would have recorded its presence.

"No. Water temperature eighty-six. Sodium chloride four-fifths Earth normal." She looked up, surprised. "Why so low?"

"More water in the ocean, maybe. Or maybe we've had a nova since we were here last."

It was getting late, almost sunset. Soon it would be time for the photographic star-charts to be made. Hugh brought himself up short and smiled bitterly. He too was in the grip of habit. Still, why not? Perhaps they could estimate, somehow, how many millions of years had passed.

Why? What good would it do them to find out?

After a while the sun set and a little later the full moon rose, hazy and indistinct behind the clouds of water vapor. Hugh stared at it, watched it rise higher until it cleared the horizon, a great bloated bulk. Then he sighed and shook his head to clear it and started to work. The clouds were thick. He had to move the screening adjustment almost to its last notch before the vapor patterns blocked out and the stars were bright and unwavering and ready to be photographed. He inserted the first plate and snapped the picture of the stars whose names he knew but whose patterns were wrong, some subtly, some blatantly.

There was something he was overlooking. Some other factor, not taken into account. He developed the first plates and compared them with the star charts of Earth as it had been before they left it, and he shook his head. Whatever the factor was, it eluded him. He went back to work.

"Oh, here you are, Hugh."

He jumped at the sound of Carhill's voice. He had been working almost completely by habit, slowly swinging the telescope across the sky and snapping the plates. And trying to think.

"Why waste time on that?" Carhill added bitterly. "Who's ever going to see our records now?"

Behind Carhill, several of the other old ones nodded. Hugh was surprised that they had managed to come back to the ship without his hearing them. But of course they had come back in at sundown, as usual on a routine check, and now they were gathering to compile their reports. Hugh looked from face to face, wondering if he too was as numb and dazed and haggard appearing as they were. He probably was.

"What do you suggest, Amos?" he said.

"I say there's no use going on," Carhill said flatly. "You've all run your tests. And what have you found? No fossils. Not even a single-celled life form in the ocean. No way even to tell how many millions of years it's been."

"Maybe it hasn't been so long," Haines said. "Maybe something happened here fairly recently, and the people all went to some other system—to one of the Centauri planets, maybe."

Amos Carhill laughed bitterly. "You can say that in the face of the evidence? We *know* that millions of years have passed. Nothing's the same. Even the tides are three times what they were. It's obvious what happened. The sun novaed. Novaed and cooled. Do you really believe that our race has lasted that long, on some nearby system?"

*   *   *   *   *

His voice rose. He glared about at the others. He threw back his head suddenly and laughed, and the laughter echoed and re-echoed off the steel walls.

"I say let's die now!" Carhill cried. "There's no use going on. Hugh was right, as usual. We shouldn't have tried to come back. We've been fools, all these years, thinking we had a world to come home to."

The people muttered, crowded closer. They pushed into the observation room, shoved nearer to it in the outside corridor. They muttered in a rising note of panic as the numbing shock that gripped them gave way.

"Why not die here?" Martha Carhill's voice rose shrill above the sound of her husband's laughter. "We should have died here millions of years ago!"

Hugh McCann looked at her and at Amos and at all the others. He sighed. Why not? Why go on? There was no answer. Even a pragmatist gave up eventually, when the facts were all against him.

He glanced down at the reports on the table. All the routine reports, gathered together into routine form, written up in routine terminology. Reports on an Earth-type planet that just happened to be the Earth itself.

And then, quite suddenly, the obvious, satisfactory answer came to him. The factors clicked into place, and he wondered why he hadn't thought of them long ago. He looked up from the reports, at the people on the verge of panic, and he knew what to say to quiet them. He had the factors now.

"No!" he cried. "You're wrong. There's no reason at all to assume that our race is dead!"

Amos Carhill stopped laughing and stared at him and the others stared also and none of them believed him at all.

"It's simple!" he cried. "Why has so much time passed outside the ship while to us only fifty-three years have gone by?"

"Because we traveled too fast," Carhill said flatly. "That's why."

"Yes," Hugh said softly. "But there's one thing we've been forgetting. What we did, others could do also. Probably lots of expeditions started out after we left, all trying for the speed of light."

They stared at him. Slowly the dazed look died out of their eyes as they realized what he meant, and what the concept might mean to them. The concept of other ships, following them out into time. The concept of other men, also millions of years from the Earth they had left.

"You mean," Carhill said slowly, "that you believe other people got caught in the same trap we did—that there may be others *in this time also*?"

Hugh nodded. "Why not? Maybe they colonized some of those Earth-type planets we checked on. Anyway, we can look for them."

"No." Carhill shook his head. "If any of them had started after us we would have crossed their paths already. We never have. We never found a trace of any other expedition. Even if there is another, even if there are colonies somewhere, we could spend another fifty years looking."

"Well," Martha Carhill whispered. "Why not? It would give us something to look for."

Hugh McCann glanced around the circle of faces and saw the new hope that came into them, the new belief that sprang into existence so quickly because they wanted to believe. He smiled, somewhat sadly, and picked up the pile of reports and the photographs he had just developed.

Then he slipped out of the room, through the crowd outside, away from them and the rising hum of their voices. He didn't need to say anything more. The ship would go on.

*   *   *   *   *

"Hugh, is that you?"

"Yes, Nora."

She was waiting for him in the corridor. She came up to him and smiled and slipped her arm through his. They walked on together, down the hall past the last of the people.

"I heard what you said, Hugh. You convinced them."

He nodded. "I wonder why it took me so long to think of it."

The voices died away behind them. They were all alone. They rounded a corner where a viewscreen picked up the image of the moon, so familiar, now the only thing that was familiar about this Earth. Nora shivered.

"You were very logical, Hugh. But I didn't believe you."

He glanced around and saw that there was no one near them and that the communicators in this part of the ship were turned off. Only then did he answer her.

"I didn't believe myself, Nora."

"Tell me."

"When we're outside."

They went down the winding ramp that led to the interior of the ship. It too was deserted now. They left the carpeted, muffled corridors and their footsteps rang on the steel plates that lay down the middle of the ship, its heart, where the energy converters were, and the disposal units, and the plant rooms, and the great glass spheres of the hydroponics tanks.

"It's ironic, isn't it?" Nora said slowly. "We left here so long ago, looking for worlds with life, and we come back to find our own world dead."

"It's ironic, all right." He walked along the row of tanks until he came to the one he was searching for, and then he picked up a glass cylinder and filled it from the tank.

"I had to tell them something, Nora. They couldn't have gone on, otherwise."

The bottle was full. He stoppered it and then turned away. They crossed to the nearest lock and he pushed the button that opened it. They waited a few minutes until the door came open, and then they went out, down the ramp to the ground, across the slippery rocks. Even through the clouds there was enough light to see by.

"It's warm," she said.

"It always is, now."

They were approaching the ocean. The surf beat loudly in their ears. The spray was warm against their faces, almost as warm as the night wind.

"Tell me," she said. "You know what really happened, don't you?"

"I think so. I can't really be sure."

They paused on the low ledge where he had stood earlier and watched the girls gather their data for the reports. At their feet the waves washed up to the edges of the tide pools, eddying into and out of them softly. The water looked dark and cold, but they knew that it too was warm.

"There've been lots of changes, and they all fit a pattern," he said. "The temperature. The difference in salt content in the water. The higher tides. Those things could happen for several reasons. But there's only one explanation for the other changes, the ones I found on the star charts."

She waited. The water lapped in and out, reaching almost to where they stood.

"The Earth rotates faster now," he said. "And the stars are nearer. Much nearer than they were."

"Isn't that impossible?"

"How do we know? We exceeded the speed of light. Who could say what continuum that might have put us in? I remember an analogy I read once, in a layman's book on different theories of space-time. '—The future and the past, two branches of a hyperbola, each with the speed of light as its limit—'"

"You mean," she whispered, "that we're not in the future at all? We're in the past—the far past—before there was any life on Earth?"

*   *   *   *   *

He looked down at the pools of water at their feet, the lifeless water that according to all their old discarded theories should have been teeming with life. He nodded slowly and lifted the glass cylinder he had brought from the ship and stared at it.

"That bottle," she whispered. "You filled it with bacteria, didn't you?"

He nodded again.

"You're mad, Hugh. You can't mean that *that bottle* is the origin of life on Earth! You can't."

"Maybe this isn't our Earth, Nora. Maybe there are thousands of continuums and thousands of Earths, all waiting for a ship to land someday and give them life."

Slowly he unstoppered the cylinder and knelt down at the water's edge. For a minute he paused, wondering if there were other continuums or only this one, wondering just how deep the paradox lay. Then he tipped the bottle up and poured, and the liquid from the cylinder ran down into the tide pools and eddied there and was lost in the liquid of the ocean. He poured until the bottle was empty and all the single-celled bacteria from the ship's tank mingled with the warm, lifeless waters.

The water temperatures were the same. Everything was the same, and the conditions were very favorable and the bacteria would divide and redivide and keep on dividing for millions of years.

"We'll hold the ship under light speed," he said. "And in a few million years we can drop back here and see how evolution is getting along."

He stood up and she took his hand and moved closer to him. They were both shivering, despite the warmth of the air.

"But how did life originate in the beginning?" she asked suddenly.

Hugh McCann shook his head in the darkness. "I don't know. We've been all over the galaxy and haven't found life anywhere. Perhaps it can't have a natural cause. Perhaps it's always planted. A closed circle from beginning to end."

"But something—someone—must have started the circle. Who?"

He looked down at the empty cylinder that he had dropped at the water's edge and then he looked out at the ocean, lifeless no longer. And once again he shook his head.

"We did, Nora. We're the beginning."

For a long moment their eyes met and held, and then they turned and walked away from the ocean, back toward the ship, and the people. And the moonlight glinted off the empty bottle.

THE VERY SECRET AGENT

ILLUSTRATED BY ED EMSH
ORIGINALLY PUBLISHED IN *IF WORLDS OF SCIENCE FICTION*,
NOVEMBER 1954

The Very Secret Agent

In their ship just beyond the orbit of Mars the two aliens sat looking at each other.

"No," Riuku said. "I haven't had any luck. And I can tell you right now that I'm not going to have any, and no one else is going to have any either. The Earthmen are too well shielded."

"You contacted the factory?" Nagor asked.

"Easily. It's the right one. The parking lot attendant knows there's a new weapon being produced in there. The waitress at the Jumbo Burger Grill across the street knows it. Everybody I reached knows it. But not one knows anything about what it is."

Nagor looked out through the ports of the spaceship, which didn't in the least resemble an Earth spaceship, any more than what Nagor considered sight resembled the corresponding Earth sense perception. He frowned.

"What about the research scientists? We know who some of them are. The supervisors? The technicians?"

"No," Riuku said flatly. "They're shielded. Perfectly I can't make contact with a single mind down there that has the faintest inkling of what's going on. We never should have let them develop the shield."

"Have you tried contacting everyone? What about the workers?"

"Shielded. All ten thousand of them. Of course I haven't checked all of them yet, but—"

"Do it," Nagor said grimly. "We've got to find out what that weapon is. Or else get out of this solar system."

Riuku sighed. "I'll try," he said.

*   *   *   *   *

Someone put another dollar in the juke box, and the theremins started in on Mare Indrium Mary for the tenth time since Pete Ganley had come into the bar. "Aw shut up," he said, wishing there was some way to turn them off. Twelve-ten. Alice got off work at Houston's at twelve. She ought to be here by now. She would be, if it weren't Thursday. Shield boosting night for her.

Why, he asked himself irritably, couldn't those scientists figure out some way to keep the shields up longer than a week? Or else why didn't they have boosting night the same for all departments? He had to stay late every Friday and Alice every Thursday, and all the time there was Susan at home ready to jump him if he wasn't in at a reasonable time....

"Surprised, Pete?" Alice Hendricks said at his elbow.

He swung about, grinned at her. "Am I? You said it. And here I was about to go. I never thought you'd make it before one." His grin faded a little. "How'd you do it? Sweet-talk one of the guards into letting you in at the head of the line?"

She shook her bandanaed head, slid onto the stool beside him and crossed her knees—a not very convincing sign of femininity in a woman wearing baggy denim coveralls. "Aren't you going to buy me a drink, honey?"

"Oh, sure." He glanced over at the bartender. "Another beer. No, make it two." He pulled the five dollars out of his pocket, shoved it across the bar, and looked back at Alice, more closely this time. The ID badge, pinned to her hip. The badge, with her name, number, department, and picture—and the little meter that measured the strength of her Mind Shield.

The dial should have pointed to full charge. It didn't. It registered about seventy per cent loss.

Alice followed his gaze. She giggled. "It was easy," she said. "The guards don't do more than glance at us, you know. And everyone who's supposed to go through Shielding on Thursday has the department number stamped on a yellow background. So all I did was make a red background, like yours, and slip it on in the restroom at Clean-up time."

"But Alice...." Pete Ganley swallowed his beer and signaled for another. "This is serious. You've got to keep the shields up. The enemy is everywhere. Why, right now, one could be probing you."

"So what? The dial isn't down to Danger yet. And tomorrow I'll just put the red tag back on over the yellow one and go through Shielding in the same line with you. They won't notice." She giggled again. "I thought it was smart, Petey. You oughta think so too. You know why I did it, don't you?"

Her round, smooth face looked up at him, wide-eyed and full-lipped. She had no worry wrinkles like Susan's, no mouth pulled down at the corners like Susan's, and under that shapeless coverall....

"Sure, baby, I'm glad you did it," Pete Ganley said huskily.

Riuku was glad too, the next afternoon when the swing shift started pouring through the gates.

It was easy, once he'd found her. He had tested hundreds, all shielded, some almost accessible to him, but none vulnerable enough. Then this one came. The shield was so far down that contact was almost easy. Painful, tiring, but not really difficult. He could feel her momentary sense of alarm, of nausea, and then he was through, integrated with her, his thoughts at home with her thoughts.

He rested, inside her mind.

"Oh, hi, Joan. No, I'm all right. Just a little dizzy for a moment. A hangover? Of course not. Not on a Friday."

Riuku listened to her half of the conversation. Stupid Earthman. If only she'd start thinking about the job. Or if only his contact with her were better. If he could use her sense perceptions, see through her eyes, hear through her ears, feel through her fingers, then everything would be easy. But he couldn't. All he could do was read her thoughts. Earth thoughts at that....

... The time clock. Where's my card? Oh, here it is. Only 3:57. Why did I have to hurry so? I had lots of time....

"Why, Mary, how nice you look today. That's a new hairdo, isn't it? A permanent? Yeah, what kind?" ... *What a microbe! Looks like pink straw, her hair does, and of course she thinks it's beautiful....* "I'd better get down to my station. Old Liverlips will be ranting again. You oughta be glad you have Eddie for a lead man. Eddie's cute. So's Dave, over in 77. But Liverlips, ugh...."

She was walking down the aisle to her station now. A procession of names: *Maisie, and Edith, and that fat slob Natalie, and if Jean Andrews comes around tonight flashing that diamond in my face again, I'll—I'll kill her....*

"Oh hello, Clinton. What do you mean, late? The whistle just blew. Of course I'm ready to go to work." *Liverlips, that's what you are. And still in that same blue shirt. What a wife you must have. Probably as sloppy as you are....*

Good, Riuku thought. Now she'll be working. Now he'd find out whatever it was she was doing. Not that it would be important, of course, but let him learn what her job was, and what those other girls' jobs were, and in a little while he'd have all the data he needed. Maybe even before the shift ended tonight, before she went through the Shielding boost.

He shivered a little, thinking of the boost. He'd survive it, of course. He'd be too well integrated with her by then. But it was nothing to look forward to.

Still, he needn't worry about it. He had the whole shift to find out what the weapon was. The whole shift, here inside Alice's mind, inside the most closely guarded factory on or under or above the surface of the Earth. He settled down and waited, expectantly.

Alice Hendricks turned her back on the lead man and looked down the work table to her place. The other girls were there already. Lois and Marge and Coralie, the other three members of the Plug table, Line 73.

"Hey, how'd you make out?" Marge said. She glanced around to make sure none of the lead men or timekeepers were close enough to overhear her, then went on. "Did you get away with it?"

"Sure," Alice said. "And you should of seen Pete's face when I walked in."

She took the soldering iron out of her locker, plugged it in, and reached out for the pan of 731 wires. "You know, it's funny. Pete's not so good looking, and he's sort of a careless dresser and all that, but oh, what he does to me." She filled the 731 plug with solder and reached for the white, black, red wire.

"You'd better watch out," Lois said. "Or Susan's going to be doing something to you."

"Oh, her." Alice touched the tip of the iron to the solder filled pin, worked the wire down into position. "What can she do? Pete doesn't give a damn about her."

"He's still living with her, isn't he?" Lois said.

Alice shrugged.... *What a mealy-mouthed little snip Lois could be, sometimes. You'd think to hear her that she was better than any of them, and luckier too, with her Joe and the kids. What a laugh! Joe was probably the only guy who'd ever looked at her, and she'd hooked him right out of school, and now with three kids in five years and her working nights....*

Alice finished soldering the first row of wires in the plug and started in on the second. So old Liverlips thought she wasted time, did he? Well, she'd show him. She'd get out her sixteen plugs tonight.

"Junior kept me up all night last night," Lois said. "He's cutting a tooth."

"Yeah," Coralie said, "It's pretty rough at that age. I remember right after Mike was born...."

Don't they ever think of anything but their kids? Alice thought. She stopped listening to them. She heard Pete's voice again, husky and sending little chills all through her, and his face came between her and the plug and the white green wire she was soldering. His face, with those blue eyes that went right through a girl and that little scar that quirked up the corner of his mouth....

"Oh, oh," Alice said suddenly. "I've got solder on the outside of the pin." She looked around for the alcohol.

Riuku probed. Her thoughts were easy enough to read, but just try to translate them into anything useful.... He probed deeper. The plugs she was soldering. He could get a good picture of them, of the wires, of the harness lacing that Coralie was doing. But it meant nothing. They could be making anything. Radios, monitor units, sound equipment.

Only they weren't. They were making a weapon, and this bit of electronic equipment was part of that weapon. What part? What did the 731 plug do?

Alice Hendricks didn't know. Alice Hendricks didn't care.

The first break. Ten minutes away from work. Alice was walking back along the aisle that separated Assembly from the men's Machine Shop. A chance, perhaps. She was looking at the machines, or rather past them, at the men.

"Hello, Tommy. How's the love life?" He's not bad at all. Real cute. Though not like Pete, oh no.

The machines. Riuku prodded at her thoughts, wishing he could influence them, wishing that just for a moment he could see, hear, feel, *think* as she would never think.

The machines were—machines. That big funny one where Ned works, and Tommy's spot welder, and over in the corner where the superintendent is—he's a snappy dresser, tie and everything.

The corner. Restricted area. Can't go over. High voltage or something....

Her thoughts slid away from the restricted area. Should she go out for lunch or eat off the sandwich machine? And Riuku curled inside her mind and cursed her with his rapidly growing Earthwoman's vocabulary.

At the end of the shift he had learned nothing. Nothing about the weapon, that is. He had found out a good deal about the sex life of Genus Homo—information that made him even more glad than before that his was a one-sexed race.

*   *   *   *   *

With work over and tools put away and Alice in the restroom gleefully thinking about the red Friday night tag she was slipping onto her ID badge, he was as far from success as ever. For a moment he considered leaving her, looking for another subject. But he'd probably not be able to find one. No, the only thing to do was stay with her, curl deep in her mind and go through the Shielding boost, and later on....

The line. Alice's nervousness.... *Oh, oh, there's that guy with the meter—the one from maintenance. What's he want?*

"Whaddya mean, my shield's low? How could it be?" ... *If he checks the tag I'll be fired for sure. It's a lot of nonsense anyway. The enemy is everywhere, they keep telling us. Whoever saw one of them?* "No, honest, I didn't notice anything. Can I help it if.... It's okay, huh? It'll pass...."

Down to fifteen per cent, the guy said. Well, that's safe, I guess. Whew.

"Oh, hello, Paula. Whatcha talking about, what am I doing here tonight? Shut up...."

And then, in the midst of her thoughts, the pain, driving deep into Riuku, twisting at him, wrenching at him, until there was no consciousness of anything at all.

He struggled back. He was confused, and there was blankness around him, and for a moment he thought he'd lost contact altogether. Then he came into focus again. Alice's thoughts were clearer than ever suddenly. He could feel her emotions; they were a part of him now. He smiled. The Shielding boost had helped him. Integration—much more complete integration than he had ever known before.

"But Pete, honey," Alice said. "What did you come over to the gate for? You shouldn't of done it."

"Why not? I wanted to see you."

"What if one of Susan's pals sees us?"

"So what? I'm getting tired of checking in every night, like a baby. Besides, one of her pals did see us, last night, at the bar."

Fear. What'll she do? Susan's a hellcat. I know she is. But maybe Pete'll get really sick and tired of her. He looks it. He looks mad. I'd sure hate to have him mad at me....

"Let's go for a spin, baby. Out in the suburbs somewhere. How about it?"

"Well—why sure, Pete...."

Sitting beside him in the copter. *All alone up here. Real romantic, like something on the video. But I shouldn't with him married, and all that. It's not right. But it's different, with Susan such a mean thing. Poor Petey....*

Riuku prodded. He found it so much easier since the Shielding boost. If only these Earthmen were more telepathic, so that they could be controlled directly. Still, perhaps with this new integration he could accomplish the same results. He prodded again.

"Pete," Alice said suddenly. "What are we working on, anyway?"

"What do you mean, working on?" He frowned at her.

"At the plant. All I ever do is sit there soldering plugs, and no one ever tells me what for."

"Course not. You're not supposed to talk about any part of the job except your own. You know that. The slip of a lip—"

"Can cost Earth a ship. I know. Quit spouting poster talk at me, Pete Ganley. The enemy isn't even human. And there aren't any around here."

Pete looked over at her. She was pouting, the upper lip drawn under the lower. Someone must have told her that was cute. Well, so what—it was cute.

"What makes you think I know anything more than you do?" he said.

"Well, gee." She looked up at him, so near to her in the moonlight that she wondered why she wanted to talk about the plant anyway. "You're in Final Assembly, aren't you? You check the whatsits before they go out."

"Sure," he said. No harm in telling her. No spies now, not in this kind of war. Besides, she was too dumb to know anything.

"It's a simple enough gadget," Pete Ganley said. "A new type of force field weapon that the enemy can't spot until it hits them. They don't even know there's an Earth ship within a million miles, until *Bingo!*...."

She drank it in, and in her mind Riuku did too. Wonderful integration, wonderful. Partial thought control. And now, he'd learn the secret....

"You really want to know how it works?" Pete Ganley said. When she nodded he couldn't help grinning. "Well, it's analogous to the field set up by animal neurones, in a way. You've just got to damp that field, and not only damp it but blot it out, so that the frequency shows nothing at all there, and then—well, that's where those Corcoran assemblies you're soldering on come in. You produce the field...."

Alice Hendricks listened. For some reason she wanted to listen. She was really curious about the field. But, gee, how did he expect her to understand all that stuff? He sounded like her algebra teacher, or was it chemistry? Lord, how she'd hated school. Maybe she shouldn't have quit.

... Corcoran fields. E and IR and nine-space something or other. She'd never seen Pete like this before. He looked real different. Sort of like a professor, or something. He must be real smart. And so—well, not good-looking especially but, well, appealing. Real SA, he had....

"So that's how it works," Pete Ganley said. "Quite a weapon, against them. It wouldn't work on a human being, of course." She was staring at him dreamy-eyed. He laughed. "Silly, I bet you haven't understood a word I said."

"I have too."

"Liar." He locked the automatic pilot on the copter and held out his arms. "Come here, you."

"Oh, Petey...."

Who cared about the weapon? He was right, even if she wouldn't admit it. She hadn't even listened, hardly. She hadn't understood.

And neither had Riuku.

*   *   *   *   *

Riuku waited until she'd fallen soundly asleep that night before he tried contacting Nagor. He'd learned nothing useful. He'd picked up nothing in her mind except more thoughts of Pete, and gee, maybe someday they'd get married, if he only had guts enough to tell Susan where to get off....

But she was asleep at last. Riuku was free enough of her thoughts to break contact, partially of course, since if he broke it completely he wouldn't be able to get back through the Shielding. It was hard enough to reach out through it. He sent a painful probing feeler out into space, to the spot where Nagor and the others waited for his report.

"Nagor...."

"Riuku? Is that you?"

"Yes. I've got a contact. A girl. But I haven't learned anything yet that can help us."

"Louder, Riuku. I can hardly hear you...."

Alice Hendricks stirred in her sleep. The dream images slipped through her subconscious, almost waking her, beating against Riuku.

Pete, baby, you shouldn't be like that....

Riuku cursed the bisexual species in their own language.

"Riuku!" Nagor's call was harsh, urgent. "You've got to find out. We haven't much time. We lost three more ships today, and there wasn't a sign of danger. No Earthman nearby, no force fields, nothing. You've got to find out why." Those ships just disappeared.

Riuku forced his way up through the erotic dreams of Alice Hendricks. "I know a little," he said. "They damp their thought waves somehow, and keep us from spotting the Corcoran field."

"Corcoran field? What's that?"

"I don't know." Alice's thoughts washed over him, pulling him back into complete integration, away from Nagor, into a medley of heroic Petes with gleaming eyes and clutching hands and good little Alices pushing them away—for the moment.

"But surely you can find out through the girl," Nagor insisted from far away, almost out of phase altogether.

"No, Pete!" Alice Hendricks said aloud.

"Riuku, you're the only one of us with any possible sort of contact. You've got to find out, if we're to stay here at all."

"Well," Alice Hendricks thought, "maybe...."

Riuku cursed her again, in the lingua franca of a dozen systems. Nagor's voice faded. Riuku switched back to English.

*   *   *   *   *

Saturday. Into the plant at 3:58. Jean's diamond again.... *Wish it would choke her; she's got a horsey enough face for it to. Where's old Liverlips? Don't see him around. Might as well go to the restroom for a while....*

That's it, Riuku thought. Get her over past the machine shop, over by that Restricted Area. There must be something there we can go on....

"Hello, Tommy," Alice Hendricks said. "How's the love life?"

"It could be better if someone I know would, uh, cooperate...."

She looked past him, toward the corner where the big panels were with all the dials and the meters and the chart that was almost like the kind they drew pictures of earthquakes on. What was it for, anyway? And why couldn't anyone go over to it except those longhairs? High voltage her foot....

"What're you looking at, Alice?" Tommy said.

"Oh, that." She pointed. "Wonder what it's for? It doesn't look like much of anything, really."

"I wouldn't know. I've got something better to look at."

"Oh, *you!*"

Compared to Pete, he didn't have anything, not anything at all.

... Pete. Gee, he must have got home awful late last night. Wonder what Susan said to him. Why does he keep taking her lip, anyway?

Riuku waited. He prodded. He understood the Restricted Area as she understood it—which was not at all. He found out some things about the 731 plugs—that a lot of them were real crummy ones the fool day shift girls had set up wrong, and besides she'd rather solder on the 717's any day. He got her talking about the weapon again, and he found out what the other girls thought about it.

Nothing.

Except where else could you get twelve-fifty an hour soldering?

She was stretched out on the couch in the restroom lobby taking a short nap—on company time, old Liverlips being tied up with the new girls down at the other end of the line—when Riuku finally managed to call Nagor again.

"Have you found out anything, Riuku?"

"Not yet."

Silence. Then: "We've lost another ship. Maybe you'd better turn her loose and come on back. It looks as if we'll have to run for it, after all."

Defeat. The long, interstellar search for another race, a race less technologically advanced than this one, and all because of a stupid Earth female.

"Not yet, Nagor," he said. "Her boy friend knows. I'll find out. I'll make her listen to him."

"Well," Nagor said doubtfully. "All right. But hurry. We haven't much time at all."

"I'll hurry," Riuku promised. "I'll be back with you tonight."

That night after work Pete Ganley was waiting outside the gate again. Alice spotted his copter right away, even though he had the lights turned way down.

"Gee, Pete, I didn't think...."

"Get in. Quick."

"What's the matter?" She climbed in beside him. He didn't answer until the copter had lifted itself into the air, away from the factory landing lots and the bright overhead lights and the home-bound workers.

"It's Susan, who else," he said grimly. "She was really sounding off today. She kept saying she had a lot of evidence and I'd better be careful. And, well, I sure didn't want you turning up at the bar tonight of all nights."

He didn't sound like Pete.

"Why?" Alice said. "Are you afraid she'll divorce you?"

"Oh, Alice, you're as bad as—look, baby, don't you see? It would be awful for you. All the publicity, the things she'd call you, maybe even in the papers...."

He was staring straight ahead, his hands locked about the controls. He was sort of—well, distant. Not her Petey any more. Someone else's Pete. Susan's Pete....

"I think we should be more careful," he said.

Riuku twisted his way through her thoughts, tried to push them down.... *Does he love me, he's got to love me, sure he does, he just doesn't want me to get hurt....*

And far away, almost completely out of phase, Nagor's call. "Riuku, another ship's gone. You'd better come back. Bring what you've learned so far and we can withdraw from the system and maybe piece it together...."

"In a little while. Just a little while." Stop thinking about Susan, you biological schizo. Change the subject. You'll never get anything out of that man by having hysterics....

"I suppose," Alice cried bitterly, "you've been leading me on all the time. You don't love me. You'd rather have *her*!"

"That's not so. Hell, baby...."

He's angry. He's not even going to kiss me. I'm just cutting my own throat when I act like that....

"Okay, Pete. I'm sorry. I know it's tough on you. Let's have a drink, okay? Still got some in the glove compartment?"

"Huh? Oh, sure."

She poured two drinks, neat, and he swallowed his with one impatient gulp. She poured him another.

*   *   *   *   *

Riuku prodded. The drink made his job easier. Alice's thoughts calmed, swirled away from Susan and what am I going to do and why didn't I pick up with some single guy, anyway? A single guy, like Tommy maybe. Tommy and his spot welder, over there by the Restricted Area. The Restricted Area....

"Pete."

"Yeah, baby?"

"How come they let so much voltage loose in the plant, so we can't even go over in the Restricted Area?"

"Whatever made you think of that?" He laughed suddenly. He turned to her, still laughing. He was the old Pete again, she thought, with his face happy and his mouth quirked up at the corner. "Voltage loose ... oh, baby, baby. Don't you know what that is?"

"No. What?"

"That's the control panel for one of the weapons, silly. It's only a duplicate, actually—a monitor station. But it's tuned to the frequencies of all the ships in this sector and—"

She listened. She wanted to listen. She had to want to listen, now.

"Nagor, I'm getting it," Riuku called. "I'll bring it all back with me. Just a minute and I'll have it."

"How does it work, honey?" Alice Hendricks said.

"You really want to know? Okay. Now the Corcoran field is generated between the ships and areas like that one, only a lot more powerful, by—"

"It's coming through now, Nagor."

"—a very simple power source, once you get the basics of it. You—oh, oh!" He grabbed her arm. "Duck, Alice!"

A spotlight flashed out of the darkness, turned on them, outlined them. A siren whirred briefly, and then another copter pulled up beside them and a loudspeaker blared tinnily.

"Okay, bud, pull down to the landing lane."

The police.

Police. Fear, all the way through Alice's thoughts, all the way through Riuku. Police. Earth law. That meant— it must mean he'd been discovered, that they had some other means of protection besides the Shielding....

"Nagor! I've been discovered!"

"Come away then, you fool!"

He twisted, trying to pull free of Alice's fear, away from the integration of their separate terrors. But he couldn't push her thoughts back from his. She was too frightened. He was too frightened. The bond held.

"Oh, Pete, Pete, what did you do?"

He didn't answer. He landed the copter, stepped out of it, walked back to the other copter that was just dropping down behind him. "But officer, what's the matter?"

Alice Hendricks huddled down in the seat, already seeing tomorrow's papers, and her picture, and she wasn't

really photogenic, either.... And then, from the other
copter, she heard the woman laugh.

"Pete Ganley, you fall for anything, don't you?"

"Susan!"

"You didn't expect me to follow you, did you? Didn't it
ever occur to you that detectives could put a bug in your
copter? My, what we've been hearing!"

"Yeah," the detective who was driving said. "And
those pictures we took last night weren't bad either."

"Susan, I can explain everything...."

"I'm sure you can, Pete. You always try. But as for
you—you little—"

Alice ducked down away from her. Pictures. Oh God,
what it would make her look like. Still, this hag with the
pinched up face who couldn't hold a man with all the
cosmetics in the drugstore to camouflage her—she had
her nerve, yelling like that.

"Yeah, and I know a lot about you too!" Alice
Hendricks cried.

"Why, let me get my hands on you...."

"Riuku!"

Riuku prodded. Calm down, you fool. You're not
gaining anything this way. Calm down, so I can get out of
here....

Alice Hendricks stopped yelling abruptly.

"That's better," Susan said. "Pete, your taste in
women gets worse each time. I don't know why I always
take you back."

"I can explain everything."

"Oh, Pete," Alice Hendricks whispered. "Petey, you're
not—"

"Sure he is," Susan Ganley said. "He's coming with
me. The nice detectives will take you home, dear. But I
don't think you'd better try anything with them—they're
not your type. They're single."

"Pete...." But he wouldn't meet Alice's eyes. And when
Susan took his arm, he followed her.

"How could you do it, Petey...." Numb whispers, numb thoughts, over and over, but no longer frightened, no longer binding on Riuku.

Fools, he thought. Idiotic Earthmen. If it weren't for your ridiculous reproductive habits I'd have found out everything. As it is.... "Nagor, I'm coming! I didn't get anything. This woman—"

"Well, come on then. We're leaving. Right now. There'll be other systems."

Petey, Petey, Petey....

Contact thinned as he reached out away from her, toward Nagor, toward the ship. He fought his way out through the Shielding, away from her and her thoughts and every detestable thing about her. Break free, break free....

"What's the matter, Riuku? Why don't you come? Have the police caught you?"

The others were fleeing, getting farther away even as he listened to Nagor's call. Contact was hard to maintain now; he could feel communication fading.

"Riuku, if you don't come now...."

He fought, but Alice's thoughts were still with him; Alice's tears still kept bringing him back into full awareness of her.

"Riuku!"

"I—I can't!"

The Shielding boost, that had integrated him so completely with Alice Hendricks, would never let him go.

"Oh, Petey, I've lost you...."

And Nagor's sad farewell slipped completely out of phase, leaving him alone, with her.

The plant. The Restricted Area. The useless secret of Earth's now unneeded weapon. Alice Hendricks glancing past it, at the spot welding machine, at Tommy.

"How's the love life?"

"You really interested in finding out, Alice?"

"Well—maybe—"

And Riuku gibbered unheard in her mind.

THE FIRST DAY OF SPRING

ILLUSTRATED BY ED EMSH
ORIGINALLY PUBLISHED IN *FUTURE COMBINED WITH SCIENCE FICTION
STORIES,*
SEPTEMBER 1951

The First Day of Spring

The First Day of spring, the man at the weather tower had said, and certainly it felt like spring, with the cool breeze blowing lightly about her and a faint new clover smell borne in from the east. Spring—that meant they would make the days longer now, and the nights shorter, and they would warm the whole world until it was summer again.

Trina laughed aloud at the thought of summer, with its picnics and languid swims in the refilled lakes, with its music and the heavy scent of flowers and the visitors in from space for the festival. She laughed, and urged her horse faster, out of its ambling walk into a trot, a canter, until the wind streamed about her, blowing back her hair, bringing tears to her eyes as she rode homeward toward the eastern horizon—the horizon that looked so far away but wasn't really.

"Trina!"

His voice was very close. And it was familiar, though for a moment she couldn't imagine who it might be.

"Where are you?" She had reined the horse in abruptly and now looked around her, in all directions, toward the north and south and east and west, toward the farm houses of the neighboring village, toward the light tower and the sun tower. She saw no one. No one else rode this early in the day in the pasture part of the world.

"I'm up here, Trina."

She looked up then and saw him, hovering some thirty feet off the ground in the ridiculous windmill-like craft he and his people used when they visited the world.

"Oh, hello, Max." No wonder she had known the voice. Max Cramer, down from space, down to the world, to see her. She knew, even before he dropped his craft onto the grass beside her, that he had come to see her. He couldn't have been on the world for more than the hour she'd been riding.

"You're visiting us early this year, Max. It's not festival time for three months yet."

"I know." He cut the power to the windmill blades, and they slowed, becoming sharply visible. The horse snorted and backed away. Max smiled. "This world is very—attractive."

His eyes caught hers, held them. She smiled back, wishing for the hundredth time since last summer's festival that he were one of her people, or at least a worldling, and not a man with the too white skin of space.

"It may be attractive," she said. "But you always leave it soon enough."

He nodded. "It's too confining. It's all right, for a little while, but then...."

"How can you say that?" She shook her head sadly. Already they were arguing the same old unresolvable argument, and they had scarcely greeted each other. After all his months in space they met with the same words as they had parted. She looked past him, up and out, toward the horizon that seemed so many miles away, toward the morning sun that seemed to hang far, far off in the vaulted blue dome of the sky.

"How can you even think it? About this?"

His lips tightened. "About *this*," he repeated. "A horizon you could ride to in five minutes. A world you could ride around in two hours. A sun—you really call it a sun—that you could almost reach up and pluck out of that sky of yours." He laughed. "Illusions. World of illusions."

"Well, what do you have? A ship—a tiny ship you can't get out of, with walls you can see, all around you."

"Yes, Trina, with walls we can see."

He was still smiling, watching her, and she knew that he desired her. And she desired him. But not the stars.

"You have nothing like this," she said, knowing it wouldn't do any good. She looked past him at the light tower, one of the many that formed the protective screen about her world, that made it seem great and convex, a huge flattened sphere with the sun high above, and not the swift curving steel ball that it actually was.

This was her world. It was like Earth, like the old Earth of the legends of the time before the radiation wars. And even though her mind might know the truth about the screens that refracted light and the atomic pile that was her sun, her heart knew a more human truth. This was a world. As it had been in the beginning. As it must be till the end—or until they found a new Earth, somewhere, sometime.... Max sighed. "Yes, you have your world, Trina. And it's a good one—the best of its kind I've ever visited."

"Why don't you stay here then?"

A spaceman, she thought. With all the dozens of men in my world, why did it have to be a spaceman? With all the visitors from New France and New Chile and New Australia last festival, why did it have to be him?

"I have the stars, Trina."

"We do too!" Last festival, and the warm June night, heavy, druggedly heavy with honeysuckle and magnolia, and the hidden music from the pavillions. And Max Cramer, tall and strong boned and alien, holding her in his arms, dancing her away from her people, out onto the terrace above the little stream, beneath the full festival moon and the summer stars, the safe, sane, well ordered constellations that their ancestors had looked upon from Earth.

"My stars are real, Trina."

She shook her head, unable to argue with him. World-woman and spaceman, and always different, with nothing in common between them, really, except a brief forgetfulness at festival time.

"Come with me, Trina."

"No." She gathered up the reins and chucked at the horse and turned, slowly, for the village.

"You wouldn't come—for me?"

"You wouldn't stay, would you?"

She heard the windmill blades whir again, and a rustling of wind, and then he was beside her, skimming slowly along, barely off the ground, making her horse snort nervously away.

"Trina, I shouldn't tell you this, not until we've met with your councilmen. But I—I've got to."

He wasn't smiling now. There was a wild look about his face. She didn't like it.

"Captain Bernard's with the council now, giving them the news. But I wanted to see you first, to be the one who told you." He broke off, shook his head. "Yet when I found you I couldn't say anything. I guess I was afraid of what you'd answer...."

"What are you talking about?" She didn't want to look at him. It embarrassed her somehow, seeing him so eager. "What do you want to tell me?"

"About our last trip, Trina. We've found a world!"

She stared at him blankly, and his hand made a cutting gesture of impatience. "Oh, not a world like this one! A planet, Trina. And it's Earth type!"

She wheeled the horse about and stared at him. For a moment she felt excitement rise inside of her too, and then she remembered the generations of searching, and the false alarms, and the dozens of barren, unfit planets that the spacemen colonized, planets like ground-bound ships.

"Oh, Trina," Max cried, "This isn't like the others. It's a new Earth. And there are already people there. From not long after the Exodus...."

"A new Earth?" she said. "I don't believe it."

The council wouldn't either, she thought. Not after all the other new Earths, freezing cold or methane atmosphered or at best completely waterless. This would be like the others. A spaceman's dream.

"You've got to believe me, Trina," Max said. "And you've got to help make the others believe. Don't you see? You wouldn't live in space. I wouldn't live here—on this. But there, on a real planet, on a real Earth...."

Then suddenly she felt his excitement and it was a part of her, until against all reason she wanted to believe in his mad dream of a world. She laughed aloud as she caught up the reins and raced her horse homeward, toward the long vista of the horizon and the capital village beyond it, ten minutes gallop away.

*   *   *   *   *

Max and Trina came together into the council hall and saw the two groups, the roomful of worldmen and the half dozen spacemen, apart from each other, arguing. The spacemen's eyes were angry.

"A world," Captain Bernard said bitterly, "there for your taking, and you don't even want to look at it."

"How do we know what kind of world it is?" Councilman Elias leaned forward on the divan. His voice was gentle, almost pitying. "You brought no samples. No vegetation, no minerals...."

"Not even air samples," Aaron Gomez said softly. "Why?"

Bernard sighed. "We didn't want to wait," he said. "We wanted to get back here, to tell you."

"It may be a paradise world to *you*," Elias said. "But to us...."

Max Cramer tightened his grip on Trina's hand. "The fools," he said. "Talking and talking, and all the time this world drifts farther and farther away."

"It takes so much power to change course," Trina said. "And besides, you feel it. It makes you heavy."

She remembered the stories her father used to tell, about his own youth, when he and Curt Elias had turned the world to go to a planet the spaceman found. A planet with people—people who lived under glass domes, or deep below the formaldehyde poisoned surface.

"You could be there in two weeks, easily, even at your world's speed," Captain Bernard said.

"And then we'd have to go out," Elias said. "Into space."

The worldmen nodded. The women looked at each other and nodded too. One of the spacemen swore, graphically, and there was an embarrassed silence as Trina's people pretended not to have heard.

"Oh, let's get out of here." The spaceman who had sworn swore again, just as descriptively, and then grinned at the councilmen and their aloof, blank faces. "They don't want our planet. All right. Maybe New Chile...."

"Wait!" Trina said it without thinking, without intending to. She stood speechless when the others turned to face her. All the others. Her people and Max's. Curt Elias, leaning forward again, smiling at her.

"Yes, Trina?" the councilman said.

"Why don't we at least look at it? Maybe it is—what they say."

Expression came back to their faces then. They nodded at each other and looked from her to Max Cramer and back again at her, and they smiled. Festival time, their eyes said. Summer evenings, summer foolishness.

And festival time long behind them, but soon to come again.

"Your father went to space," Elias said. "We saw one of those worlds the spacemen talk of."

"I know."

"He didn't like it."

"I know that too," she said, remembering his bitter words and the nightmare times when her mother had had so much trouble comforting him, and the winter evenings when he didn't want even to go outside and see the familiar, Earth encircling stars.

He was dead now. Her mother was dead now. They were not here, to disapprove, to join with Elias and the others.

They would have hated for her to go out there.

She faltered, the excitement Max had aroused in her dying away, and then she thought of their argument, as old as their desire. She knew that if she wanted him it would have to be away from the worlds.

"At least we could look," she said. "And the spacemen could bring up samples. And maybe even some of the people for us to talk to."

Elias nodded. "It would be interesting," he said slowly, "to talk to some new people. It's been so long."

"And we wouldn't even have to land," Aaron Gomez said, "if it didn't look right."

The people turned to each other again and smiled happily. She knew that they were thinking of the men and women they would see, and all the new things to talk about.

"We might even invite some of them up for the festival," Elias said slowly. "Providing they're— courteous." He frowned at the young spaceman who had done the swearing, and then he looked back at Captain Bernard. "And providing, of course, that we're not too far away by then."

"I don't think you will be," Bernard said. "I think you'll stay."

"I think so too," Max Cramer said, moving closer to Trina. "I hope so."

Elias stood up slowly and signalled that the council was dismissed. The other people stood up also and moved toward the doors.

"We'd better see about changing the world's course," Aaron Gomez said.

No one objected. It was going to be done. Trina looked up at Max Cramer and knew that she loved him. And wondered why she was afraid.

*   *   *   *   *

It was ten days later that the world, New America, came into the gravitational influence of the planet's solar system. The automatic deflectors swung into functioning position, ready to change course, slowly and imperceptibly, but enough to take the world around the system and out into the freedom of space where it could wander on its random course. But this time men shunted aside the automatic controls. Men guided their homeland in, slowly now, toward the second planet from the sun, the one that the spacemen had said was so like Earth.

"We'll see it tomorrow," Trina said. "They'll shut off part of the light tower system then."

"Why don't they now?" Max Cramer asked her. It was just past sunset, and the stars of a dozen generations ago were just beginning to wink into view. He saw Venus, low on the horizon, and his lips tightened, and then he looked up to where he knew the new sun must be.

There was only the crescent of Earth's moon.

"Now?" Trina said. "Why should they turn the screens off now? We're still so far away. We wouldn't see anything."

"You'd see the sun," Max said. "It's quite bright, even from here. And from close up, from where the planet is, it looks just about like Earth's."

Trina nodded. "That's good," she said, looking over at the rose tints of the afterglow. "It wouldn't seem right if it didn't."

A cow lowed in the distance, and nearer, the laughing voices of children rode the evening breeze. Somewhere a dog barked. Somewhere else a woman called her family home to supper. Old sounds. Older, literally, than this world.

"What are the people like, out there?"

He looked at her face, eager and worried at the same time, and he smiled. "You'll like them, Trina," he said.

"They're like—well, they're more like *this* than anything else."

He gestured, vaguely, at the farmhouse lights ahead of them, at the slow walking figures of the young couples out enjoying the warm spring evening, at the old farmer leading his plow horse home along the path.

"They live in villages, not too different, from yours. And in cities. And on farms."

"And yet, you like it there, don't you?" she said.

He nodded. "Yes, I like it there."

"But you don't like it here. Why?"

"If you don't understand by now, Trina, I can't explain."

They walked on. Night came swiftly, crowding the rose and purple tints out of the western sky, closing in dark and cool and sweet smelling about them. Ahead, a footbridge loomed up out of the shadows. There was the sound of running water, and, on the bank not far from the bridge, the low murmuring of a couple of late lingering fishermen.

"The people live out in the open, like this?" Trina said.

"Yes."

"Not underground? Not under a dome?"

"I've told you before that it's like Earth, Trina. About the same size, even."

"*This* is about the same size, too."

"Not really. It only looks that way."

The fishermen glanced up as they passed, and then bent down over their lines again. Lucas Crossman, from Trina's town, and Jake Krakorian from the southern hemisphere, up to visit his sister Lucienne, who had just had twins....

Trina said hello to them as she passed, and found out that the twins looked just like their mother, except for Grandfather Mueller's eyes, and then she turned back to Max.

"Do people live all over the planet?"

"On most of it. The land sections, that is. Of course, up by the poles it's too cold."

"But how do they know each other?"

He stopped walking and stared at her, not understanding for a minute. Girl's laughter came from the bushes, and the soft urging voice of one of the village boys. Max looked back at the fishermen and then down at Trina and shook his head.

"They don't all know each other," he said. "They couldn't."

She thought of New Chile, where her cousin Isobelle was married last year, and New India, which would follow them soon to the planet, because Captain Bernard had been able to contact them by radio. She thought of her people, her friends, and then she remembered the spacemen's far flung ships and the homes they burrowed deep in the rock of inhospitable worlds. She knew that he would never understand why she pitied the people of this system.

"I suppose we'll see them soon," she said. "You're going to bring some of them back up in your ship tomorrow, aren't you?"

He stood quietly, looking down at her. His face was shadowed in the gathering night and his whole body was in shadow, tall and somehow alien seeming there before her.

"Why wait for them to come here, Trina?" he said. "Come down with us, in the ship, tomorrow. Come down and see for yourself what it's like."

She trembled. "No," she said.

And she thought of the ship, out away from the sky, not down on the planet yet but hanging above it, with no atmosphere to break the blackness, to soften the glare of the planet's sun, to shut out the emptiness.

"You'd hardly know you weren't here, Trina. The air smells the same. And the weight's almost the same too. Maybe a little lighter."

She nodded. "I know. If we land the world, I'll go out there. But not in the ship."

"All right." He sighed and let go his grip on her shoulders and turned to start walking back the way they had come, toward the town.

She thought suddenly of what he had just said, that she would hardly be able to tell the difference.

"It can't be so much like this," she said. "Or you couldn't like it. No matter what you say."

"Trina." His voice was harsh. "You've never been out in space, so you couldn't understand. You just don't know what your world is like, from outside, when you're coming in."

But she could picture it. A tiny planetoid, shining perhaps behind its own screens, a small, drifting, lonely sphere of rock. She trembled again. "I don't want to know," she said.

Somewhere in the meadows beyond the road there was laughter, a boy and a girl laughing together, happy in the night. Trina's fingers tightened on Max's hand and she pulled him around to face her and then clung to him, trembling, feeling the nearness of him as she held up her face to be kissed.

He held her to him. And slowly, the outside world of space faded, and her world seemed big and solid and sure, and in his arms it was almost like festival time again.

*   *   *   *   *

At noon the next day the world slowed again and changed course, going into an orbit around the planet, becoming a third moon, nearer to the surface than the others.

The people, all of those who had followed their normal day-to-day life even after New America came into the system, abandoned it at last. They crowded near the television towers, waiting for the signal which would open up some of the sky and show them the planet they circled, a great green disk, twice the apparent diameter of the legendary Moon of Earth.

Max stood beside Trina in the crowd that pressed close about his ship. He wore his spaceman's suit, and the helmet was in his hand. Soon he too would be aboard with the others, going down to the planet.

"You're sure you won't come, Trina? We'll be down in a couple of hours."

"I'll wait until we land there. If we do."

Curt Elias came toward them through the crowd. When he saw Trina he smiled and walked faster, almost briskly. It was strange to see him move like a young and active man.

"If I were younger," he said, "I'd go down there." He smiled again and pointed up at the zenith, where the blue was beginning to waver and fade as the sky screens slipped away. "This brings back memories."

"You didn't like that other world," Trina said. "Not any more than Father did."

"The air was bad there," Elias said.

The signal buzzer sounded again. The center screens came down. Above them, outlined by the fuzzy halo of the still remaining sky, the black of space stood forth, and the stars, and the great disk of the planet, with its seas and continents and cloud masses and the shadow of night creeping across it from the east.

"You see, Trina?" Max said softly.

The voices of the people rose, some alive with interest and others anxious, fighting back the planet and the unfamiliar, too bright stars. Trina clutched Max Cramer's hand, feeling again the eagerness of that first day, when he had come to tell her of this world.

"You're right," she whispered. "It *is* like Earth."

It was so much like the pictures, though of course the continents were different, and the seas, and instead of one moon there were two. Earth. A new Earth, there above them in the sky.

Elias let out his breath slowly. "Yes," he said. "It is. It's not a bit like that world we visited. Not a bit."

"When you're down there it's even more like Earth," Max said. "And all the way down you could watch it grow larger. It wouldn't be at all like open space."

At the poles of the planet snow gleamed, and cloud masses drifted across the equator. And the people looked, and pointed, their voices growing loud with eagerness.

"Why don't we land the world now?" Trina cried. "Why wait for the ship to bring people up here?"

"Landing the world would take a lot of power," Elias said. "It would be foolish to do it unless we planned on staying for quite a while." He sighed. "Though I would like to go down there. I'd like to see a really Earth type planet."

He looked at Max, and Max smiled. "Well, why not?" he said.

Elias smiled too. "After all, I've been in space once. I'll go again." He turned and pushed his way through the people.

Trina watched him go. Somehow he seemed a symbol to her. Old and stable, he had been head of the council since she was a child. And he had gone into space with her father....

"Please come, Trina," Max said. "There's nothing to be afraid of."

With both Max and Elias along, certainly it couldn't be too bad. Max was right. There was nothing, really, to be afraid of. She smiled up at him.

"All right," she said. "I'll go."

And then she was walking with Max Cramer toward the ship and trying not to remember her father crying in his sleep.

*   *   *   *   *

The ship rose, and Trina cried out as she felt the heaviness wrench her back against the cushions. Max reached over to her. She felt the needle go into her arm again, and then sank back into the half sleep that he had promised would last until they were ready to land.

When she awoke the planet was a disk no longer, but a great curving mass beneath the ship, with the mountains and valleys and towns of its people plainly visible. But the planet's sky still lay below, and around them, in every direction except down, space stretched out, blacker than any night on the world. The world. Trina moaned and closed her eyes, glad she hadn't seen it, somewhere tiny and insignificant behind them.

Max heard her moan and reached toward her. She slept again, and woke only when they were down and he was tugging the straps loose from around her. She sat up, still numbed by the drug, still half asleep and unreal feeling, and looked out about her at the planet's surface.

They were in a field of some sort of grain. Beyond the scorched land where they had come down the tall cereal grasses rippled in the soft wind, a great undulating sea of green, reaching out toward the far off hills and the horizon. Cloud shadows drifted across the fields, and the shadow of the ship reached out to meet them.

Trina rubbed her eyes in wonder.

"It *is* like the world," she said. "Just like it."

For a moment she was sure that they were back on the world again, in some momentarily unrecognized pasture, or perhaps on one of the sister worlds. Then, looking along the row of hills to where they dropped away into an extension of the plain, she saw that the horizon was a little too far, and that the light shimmered differently, somehow, than on her home. But it was such a little difference.

"Come on outside," Max Cramer said. "You'll be all right now."

She stood up and followed him. Elias was already at the airlock, moving unsteadily and a little blankly, also still partly under the influence of the narcotic.

The lock opened. Captain Bernard stepped out and went down the ladder to the ground. The others followed him. Within a few minutes the ship stood empty.

*   *   *   *   *

Trina breathed the open air of the planet and felt the warmth on her face and smelled the scent of grass and the elusive fragrance of alien flowers. She heard the song of some strange, infinitely sweet throated bird.

"It's—it's Earth," she whispered.

Voices, eager, calling voices, sang out in the distance. Then, little cars rolled toward them through the field, mowing down the grass, cutting themselves a path to the ship. People, men and women and children, were calling greetings.

"This is where we landed before," Max said. "We told them we'd be back."

They were sunbronzed, country people, and except for their strange clothing they might have been from any of the worlds. Even their language was the same, though accented differently, with some of the old, unused words, like those in the legends.

"You've brought your people?" the tall man who stood in the forefront said to Captain Bernard.

"They're up there." Bernard pointed up at the sky, and the people looked up. Trina looked up too. One of the planet's moons was almost full overhead. But the world was invisible, shut off by the sky and the clouds and the light of the earthlike sun.

"They'd like some of you to come visit their world," Bernard said. "If any of you are willing."

The tall man nodded. "Everyone will want to go," he said. "Very few ships ever land here. Until you came, it had been years."

"You'd go out in space?" Trina said incredulously.

Again the man nodded. "I was a spaceman once," he said. "All of us MacGregors were." Then he sighed.

"Sometimes even now I want to go out again. But there've been no ships here, not for years."

Trina looked past him, at the women and the children, at the lush fields and the little houses far in the distance. "You'd leave this?"

MacGregor shook his head. "No, of course not. Not to live in space permanently. I'd always come back."

"It's a fine world to come back to," Max said, and he and the tall man smiled at each other, as if they shared something that Trina couldn't possibly understand.

"We might as well go into town," MacGregor said.

They walked over to the cars. MacGregor stopped beside one of them, his hand on the door button.

"Here, let me drive." The girl stepped forward out of the crowd as she spoke. She was tall, almost as tall as MacGregor, and she had the same high cheekbones and the same laughter lines about her eyes.

"Not this time, Saari," MacGregor said. "This time you can entertain our guests." He turned to Max and Trina and smiled. "My daughter." His face was proud.

They climbed in, Trina wedging herself into the middle of the back seat between Max and the planet girl. The car throbbed into motion, then picked up speed, jolting a bit on the rough country road. The ground rushed past and the fields rushed past and Trina leaned against Max and shut her eyes against the dizzying speed. Here, close to the ground, so close that they could feel every unevenness of its surface, it was far worse than in the windmill like craft the spacemen used on the worlds.

"Don't you have cars?" Saari asked.

"No," Trina said. "We don't need them."

A car like this would rush all the way around the world in half an hour. In a car like this one even the horizons wouldn't look right, rushing to meet them. Here, though the horizons stayed the same, unmoving while the fence posts and the farmhouses and the people flashed past.

"What do you use for transportation then?"

"We walk," Trina said, opening her eyes to look at the girl and then closing them again. "Or we ride horses."

"Oh."

A few minutes later the car slowed, and Trina opened her eyes again.

"We're coming into town," Saari said.

They had climbed up over the brow of a small hill and were now dropping down. At the bottom of the hill the houses clumped together, sparsely at first, then more and more of them, so that the whole valley was filled with buildings, and more buildings hugged the far slopes.

"There are so many of them," Trina whispered.

"Oh, no, Trina. This is just a small town."

"But the people—all those people...."

They crowded the streets, watching the cars come in, looking with open curiosity at their alien visitors. Faces, a thousand faces, all different and yet somehow all alike, blended together into a great anonymous mass.

"There aren't half that many people on the whole world," Trina said.

Saari smiled. "Just wait till you see the city."

Trina shook her head and looked up at Max. He was smiling out at the town, nodding to some men he apparently knew, with nothing but eagerness in his face. He seemed a stranger. She looked around for Curt Elias, but he was in one of the other cars cut off from them by the crowd. She couldn't see him at all.

"Don't you like it?" Saari said.

"I liked it better where we landed."

Max turned and glanced down at her briefly, but his hand found hers and held it, tightly, until her own relaxed. "If you want to, Trina, we can live out there, in those fields."

For a moment she forgot the crowd and the endless faces as she looked up at him. "Do you mean that, Max? We could really live out there?"

Where it was quiet, and the sun was the same, and the birds sang sweetly just before harvest time, where she would have room to ride and plenty of pasture for her favorite horse. Where she would have Max, there with her, not out somewhere beyond the stars.

"Certainly we could live there," he said. "That's what I've been saying all along."

"You could settle down here?"

He laughed. "Oh, I suppose I'd be out in space a good deal of the time," he said. "The ships will come here now, you know. But I'll always come home, Trina. To this world. To you."

And suddenly it didn't matter that the girl beside her chuckled, nor that there were too many people crowding around them, all talking at once in their strangely accented voices. All that mattered was Max, and this world, which was real after all, and a life that seemed like an endless festival time before her.

*   *   *   *   *

Evening came quickly, too quickly, with the sun dropping in an unnatural plunge toward the horizon. Shadows crept out from the houses of the town, reached across the narrow street and blended with the walls of the houses opposite. The birds sang louder in the twilight, the notes of their song drifting in from the nearby fields. And there was another sound, that of the wind, not loud now but rising, swirling fingers of dust in the street.

Trina sat in front of the town cafe with the planet girl, Saari. Max Cramer was only a few feet away, but he paid no attention to her, and little to Elias. He was too busy telling the planet people about space.

"Your man?" Saari asked.

"Yes," Trina said. "I guess so."

"You're lucky." Saari looked over at Max and sighed, and then she turned back to Trina. "My father was a spaceman. He used to take my mother up, when they

were first married, when the ships were still running."
She sighed. "I remember the ships, a little. But it was
such a long time ago."

"I can't understand you people." Trina shook her head.
"Leaving all of this, just to go out in space."

The room was crowded, oppressively crowded.
Outside, too many people walked the shadowed streets.
Too many voices babbled together. The people of this
planet must be a little mad, Trina thought, to live cooped
together as the spacemen lived, with all their world
around them.

Saari sat watching her, and nodded. "You're different,
aren't you? From us, and from them too." She looked over
at Max and Bernard and the others, and then she looked
at Curt Elias, who sat clenching and unclenching his
hands, saying nothing.

"Yes, we're different," Trina said.

Max Cramer's voice broke incisively into the silence
that lay between them then. "I don't see why," he said,
"we didn't all know about this world. Especially if more
than one ship came here."

Saari's father laughed softly. "It's not so strange. The
ships all belonged to one clan. The MacGregors. And
eventually all of them either were lost in space
somewhere or else grew tired of roaming around and
settled down. Here." He smiled again, and his high
cheekboned face leaned forward into the light. "Like
me...."

Night. Cloudless, black, but hazed over with
atmosphere and thus familiar, not like the night of space.
The two small moons, the stars in unfamiliar places, and
somewhere, a star that was her world. And Trina sat and
listened to the planet men talk, and to the spacemen
among them who could no longer be distinguished from
the native born. Outside, in the narrow street, wind
murmured, skudding papers and brush before it, vague
shadows against the light houses. Wind, rising and

moaning, the sound coming in over the voices and the music from the cafe singers.

It was a stronger wind than ever blew on the world, even during the winter, when the people had to stay inside and wish that Earth tradition might be broken and good weather be had the year around.

"We'd better get back to the ship," Elias said.

They stopped talking and looked at him, and he looked down at his hands, embarrassed. "They'll be worried about us at home."

"No, they won't," Max said. Then he saw the thin, blue-veined hands trembling and the quiver not quite controlled in the wrinkled neck. "Though perhaps we should start back...."

Trina let out her breath in relief. To be back in the ship, she thought, with the needle and its forgetfulness, away from the noise and the crowd and the nervousness brought on by the rising wind.

It would be better, of course, when they had their place in the country. There it would be warm and homelike and quiet, with the farm animals near by, and the weather shut out, boarded out and forgotten, the way it was in winter on the world.

"You're coming with us?" Captain Bernard was saying.

"Yes, we're coming." Half a dozen of the men stood up and began pulling on their long, awkward coats.

"It'll be good to get back in space again," MacGregor said. "For a while." He smiled. "But I'm too old for a spaceman's life now."

"And I'm too old even for this," Elias said apologetically. "If we'd found this planet the other time...." He sighed and shook his head and looked out the window at the shadows that were people, bent forward, walking into the wind. He sighed again. "I don't know. I just don't know."

Saari got up and pulled on her wrap too. Then she walked over to one of the other women, spoke to her a minute, and came back carrying a quilted, rough fabricked coat. "Here, Trina, you'd better put this on. It'll be cold out."

"Are you going with us?"

"Sure. Why not? Dad's talked enough about space. I might as well see what it's like for myself."

Trina shook her head. But before she could speak, someone opened the door and the cold breeze came in, hitting her in the face.

"Come on," Saari said. "It'll be warm in the car."

Somehow she was outside, following the others. The wind whipped her hair, stung her eyes, tore at her legs. The coat kept it from her body, but she couldn't protect her face, nor shut out the low moaning wail of it through the trees and the housetops.

She groped her way into the car. The door slammed shut, and the wind retreated, a little.

"Is it—is it often like that?"

Saari MacGregor looked at her. Max Cramer turned and looked at her, and so did the others in the car. For a long moment no one said anything. And then Saari said, "Why, this is *summer*, Trina."

"Summer?" She thought of the cereal grasses, rippling in the warm day. They'd be whipping in the wind now, of course. The wind that was so much stronger than any the world's machines ever made.

"You ought to be here in winter," Saari was saying. "It really blows then. And there are the rainstorms, and snow...."

"Snow?" Trina said blankly.

"Certainly. A couple of feet of it, usually." Saari stopped talking and looked at Trina, and surprise crept even farther into her face. "You mean you don't have snow on your world?"

"Why, yes, we have snow. We have everything Earth had." But snow two feet deep ... Trina shivered, thinking of winter on the world, and the soft dusting of white on

winter mornings, the beautiful powdery flakes cool in the
sunlight.

"They have about a sixteenth of an inch of it," Max
said. "And even that's more than some of the worlds have.
It hardly ever even rains in New California."

Saari turned away finally, and the others did too. The
car started, the sound of its motors shutting out the wind
a little, and then they were moving. Yet it was even more
frightening, rushing over the roads in the darkness, with
the houses flashing past and the trees thrashing in the
wind and the people briefly seen and then left behind in
the night.

The ship was ahead. The ship. Now even it seemed a
safe, familiar place.

"This isn't like Earth after all," Trina said bitterly.
"And it seemed so beautiful at first."

Then she saw that Saari MacGregor was looking at
her again, but this time more in pity than in surprise.

"Not like Earth, Trina? You're wrong. We have a
better climate than Earth's. We never have blizzards, nor
hurricanes, and it's never too cold nor too hot, really."

"How can you say that?" Trina cried. "We've kept *our*
world like Earth. Oh, maybe we've shortened winter a
little, but still...."

Saari's voice was sad and gentle, as if she were
explaining something to a bewildered child. "My mother's
ancestors came here only a few years out from Earth,"
she said. "And do you know what they called this planet?
A paradise. A garden world."

"That's why they named it Eden," Max Cramer said.

Then they were at the ship, out of the car, running to
the airlock, with the grass lashing at their legs and the
wind lashing at their faces and the cold night air aflame
suddenly in their lungs. And Trina couldn't protest any
longer, not with the world mad about her, not with
Saari's words ringing in her ears like the wind.

She saw them carry Curt Elias in, and then Max was helping her aboard, and a moment later, finally, the airlock doors slipped shut and it was quiet.

She held out her arm for the needle.

*   *   *   *   *

When she awoke again it was morning. Morning on the world. They had carried her to one of the divans in the council hall, one near a window so that she could see the familiar fields of her homeland as soon as she awoke. She rubbed her eyes and straightened and looked up at the others. At Elias, still resting on another divan. At Captain Bernard. At Saari and her father, and another man from the planet. At Max.

He looked at her, and then sighed and turned away, shaking his head.

"Are we—are we going back there?" Trina asked.

"No," Elias said. "The people are against it."

There was silence for a moment, and then Elias went on. "I'm against it. I suppose that even if I'd been young I wouldn't have wanted to stay." His eyes met Trina's, and there was pity in them.

"No," Max said. "You wouldn't have wanted to."

"And yet," Elias said, "I went down there. Trina went down there. Her father and I both went out into space." He sighed. "The others wouldn't even do that."

"You're not quite as bad, that's all," Max said bluntly. "But I don't understand any of you. None of us ever has understood you. None of us ever will."

Trina looked across at him. Her fingers knew every line of his face, but now he was withdrawn, a stranger. "You're going back there, aren't you?" she said. And when he nodded, she sighed. "We'll never understand you either, I guess."

She remembered Saari's question of the night before, "Is he your man?" and she realized that her answer had not been the truth. She knew now that he had never been hers, not really, nor she his, that the woman who would be his would be like Saari, eager and unafraid and laughing in the wind, or looking out the ports at friendly stars.

Elias leaned forward on the divan and gestured toward the master weather panel for their part of the village, the indicators that told what it was like today and what it would be like tomorrow all over the world. "I think I understand," he said. "I think I know what we did to our environment, through the generations. But it doesn't do much good, just knowing something."

"You'll never change," Max said.

"No, I don't think we will."

Captain Bernard got up, and MacGregor got up too. They looked at Max. Slowly he turned his head and smiled at Trina, and then he too stood up. "Want to come outside and talk, Trina?"

But there was nothing to say. Nothing she could do except break down and cry in his arms and beg him not to leave her, beg him to spend the rest of his life on a world she could never leave again.

"No," she said. "I guess not." And then, the memories rushed back, and the music, and the little lane down by the stream where the magnolias spread their web of fragrance. "It's—it's almost festival time, Max. Will you be here for it?"

"I don't know, Trina."

It meant no; she knew that.

*   *   *   *   *

The weeks slipped by, until it was summer on the world, until the festival music sang through the villages and the festival flowers bloomed and the festival lovers slipped off from the dances to walk among them. There was a breeze, just enough to carry the mingled fragrances and the mingled songs, just enough to touch the throat and ruffle the hair and lie lightly between the lips of lovers.

Trina danced with Aaron Gomez, and remembered. And the wind seemed too soft somehow, almost lifeless, with the air too sweet and cloying.

She wondered what a festival on the planet would be like.

Max, with Saari MacGregor, perhaps, laughing in the wind, running in the chill of evening along some riverbank.

I could have gone with him, she thought. I could have gone....

But then the music swirled faster about them, the pulse of it pounding in her ears, and Aaron swept her closer as they danced, spinning among the people and the laughter, out toward the terrace, toward the trees with leaves unstirring in the evening air. All was color and sound and scent, all blended, hypnotically perfect, something infinitely precious that she could never, never leave.

For it was summer on the world, and festival time again.

THE HOUSE ON THE VACANT LOT

ORIGINALLY PUBLISHED IN *FANTASTIC STORY*
SUMMER, 1952

THE HOUSE ON THE VACANT LOT

"No," Ronald Brisbane said firmly, "I don't like any of these houses. They're all too much alike. No imagination."

The real estate agent sighed. It was a hot July afternoon, and both his feet and his temper were beginning to blister. "After all, Mr. Brisbane," he said, "just what can you expect for fifteen thousand dollars? This subdivision is one of the finest . . ."

Ronald Brisbane shook his head. "Birdhouses," he said. "Row after row of birdhouses. Little square boxes with pointed roofs." He peered owlishly up at the agent. "Do you really expect people to *live* in them?"

For just an instant the agent's habitually bland expression was replaced by one of frustrated mayhem, Ronald Brisbane hastily stepped back off the sidewalk onto the newly seeded lawn of House 22.

"I didn't . . ." he began, then suddenly he smiled delightedly. "Oh," he cried. "There's the very one! Funny I didn't see it before." He pointed over the realtor's shoulder.

The agent turned, puzzled. There was nothing but a vacant lot across the street in back of him. The subdivision hadn't yet built up that far. Then he gasped and stopped listening to the delighted sounds that Mr. Brisbane was making.

For there *was* a house on the opposite corner. A rambling Moorish style house set in the middle of a rose garden. A very solid and substantial looking house that just couldn't possibly be where it was.

"I'll take that one," Mr. Brisbane said, almost running as he hurried across the street.

"But it isn't . . ." the agent exclaimed after him.

Mr. Brisbane paid no attention. He stepped up onto the opposite curb and started up onto the flagstone path between the rose bushes.

"Hey, come back here!" the agent called.

Ronald Brisbane strode purposefully up to the front door. For a moment he stood fumbling with the knob, and then the agent took a half-hearted step after him. The Brisbane straightened triumphantly, walked through the door and closed it behind him.

"It's not possible," the agent whispered.

The house stood silent. The rose bushes swayed a little in the faint breeze. The scent was heavy and cloying.

The agent rubbed his hand over his eyes and forehead, wiping away the sweat. Movers could have set the house up while he was showing Brisbane the other side of the subdivision, but the garden ... He looked back towards the roses, and heard himself whimper.

Across the street was nothing but a vacant lot.

*   *   *   *   *

Just inside the door Ronald Brisbane paused and looked around.

"An interesting arrangement," he murmured. "Furnished, too."

He scuffed his toe against the nap of the wheat-colored carpet. It was soft and springy underfoot, made from some sort of spun fiber he couldn't identify.

"Quite different," he said happily. "Really designed to be lived in. Of course, it probably is a lot more than fifteen thousand . . ."

He glanced back to see if the real estate agent had come in yet, but saw no one. "That's odd," he muttered. "I wonder what's keeping him?"

For a minute he paused uncertainly, then he turned back to the front door and twisted the knob.

Nothing happened. The knob turned only so far, then caught. He rattled it several times an jerked hard on the door, but it still wouldn't open.

"Locked," he said impatiently.

He took one step towards the window. The he froze.

The incredibly bony young woman in the short yellow tunic stared back at him. Her body had tensed as she saw him, then relaxed.

"How did you get in here?" she asked.

"I—I'm terribly sorry, Miss..."

He swallowed and dropped his eyes. He found himself staring at her hemline, which was considerably above her knees, and looked up hastily. She stood watching him speculatively.

"I—I didn't know anybody lived here," he explained lamely. "I thought this house was for sale."

"Well, it's not." She looked him up and down, then shook her head with a puzzled frown. "Do you usually dress up for a costume ball when you go shopping for a house?" she asked abruptly.

"What?" Ronald Brisbane glanced down at his double breasted pin-stripe suit and solid blue tie. They weren't even mussed. He looked back at the girl and decided she must have been joking, for she would easily have won a prize for outlandish appearance at any costume party.

It wasn't so much the yellow tunic and thronged sandals—those were simple enough. But her face was a topheavy mask of thick purple eyeshadow and absolutely no lipstick. Her black hair might have been really beautiful if it hadn't been cut in straight bangs across and already too low forehead and th en piled up in long, carefully coiled ringlets pinned to the top of her head. She rubbed her cheek with one hand thoughtfully, and he noticed that her fingernails were long and silvered.

Slowly Ronald Brisbane backed toward the door through which he had entered. "I'll be going now," he said. "Sorry to have bothered you. Could you—could you let me out? I seem to have locked myself in here..."

The girl glanced idly toward a panel recessed in the wall behind her. A yellow light blinked on and off.

"Of course the door is locked," she said. "The house is moving."

Ronald Brisbane eyed her warily. She seemed calm enough, at the moment, but he really couldn't be sure... Then resolutely he crossed over to the front window and drew back the curtains.

"No," he gasped. "Oh, no!"

He dug his fingers into the yielding plastic window sill and closed his eyes. The he forced himself to open them and look out again, hoping he had been wrong, hoping that somehow he had lost track of the intervening hours and it was night outside. But it wasn't. The rose bushes were twined shadows in the haze of the garden. But beyond the garden it was black, much too black.

"What's the matter?" He heard her voice dimly, from a long way off. "Are you ill?"

He leaned his head against the window glass. It felt cool and firm, real enough in this crazy room. "What's happening?" he asked hoarsely.

"Nothing's happening," she said. "We're just moving, that's all. Junior's driving Father to work. We'll be there soon."

Just then the whole house shook gently. "We're stopping now," she said. "We're..."

The house lurched violently. Ronald Brisbane felt the window sill jerk from his hands just as the floor started to tilt...

*   *   *   *   *

"He'll be all right," a strange voice was saying. "He just got a bad bump."

Ronald Brisbane groaned.

"I think he's waking up now." It was the girl's voice.

Slowly he opened his eyes.

He saw their legs first. Two pairs of toothpicks, dead white skin and knobby knees. He winced and raised his head.

The girl in the yellow tunic smiled down at him delightedly.

"Look, Mother," she said. "He's awake now."

Ronald Brisbane pulled himself to a sitting position. "What happened ..." he began.

"Hush," said the older woman. "Don't talk now. Just rest," She smiled brightly down at him. "Get the young man a glass of water, Lilian."

"Yes, Mother," Lilian said.

He rubbed his aching head and looked again at the two women. He hadn't been mistaken. The family resemblance was very strong. Both were tall and angular. Both had long bare arms and bony wrists. Both had flat chests, thin necks, square faces, and bangs. The only difference in their dress was that the mother wore less eye shadow and her hair was gathered up into a bun instead of a pile of ringlets.

"Look," Ronald Brisbane said. "I'm either crazy or dreaming, I know. But please tell me, where am I? What happened?"

The older woman smile a bit uncomfortably. "We've just had a—a little accident with the house," she said. "Junior was driving, and he must not have been paying attention..."

"Here," Lilian said, thrusting a glass of water in front of him, "Drink this. You'll feel better."

"All I want," he said desperately, "Is to get out of here."

Lilian's mother bit her lip. "You could leave now, of course, if you're in a hurry. But I wouldn't advise it. You see, we don't know exactly where we are. Junior got off the travel lanes a bit. It might be hard for you to find a housecar back to your home."

Ronald closed his eyes again. He was beginning to feel a terrible doubt in the pit of his stomach.

"Does your head ache very badly?" Lilian asked, layer her hand gently on his forehead.

He opened his eyes again hastily. "No, it's not that," he said. "It's just that I don't know what's going on. Look, I don't even know what you're talking about. Travel lanes, house-cars—you mean you actually drive around *inside* this house?"

"Why certainly," Lilian said. "Don't you?"

"No."

"I thought everyone did," her mother said. "This is very odd. I wonder where Junior was, anyway, when he stopped this house long enough for you to come in?"

"I can tell you that," Ronald Brisbane said grimly. "He was in the United States of America..."

Lilian clapped her hands, "Oh, I remember that!" she exclaimed delightedly. "It's in all the ancient history books. So you're from Earth, too. I'm glad..."

She stopped and looked at him doubtfully. "Are you sure?" she said. "You don't look much like us. I though..."

"Lilian," her mother said reproachfully.

Lilian flushed. "I'm sorry, Mother," she said. "You get used to a person and forget..."

The older woman sighed. "I know," she said. Then she leaned over his couch and asked, "Are you really from the United States? From that long ago?"

"Yes," he said. "I was out looking for a house. It was July, 1952." He glanced down at his watch. "It was also," he added, "just about half an hour ago."

*   *   *   *   *

They both stared at him and he found himself enjoying their mingled amazement and disbelief. He was quite sure that anything anyone said now would be anticlimactic.

He was wrong. The kilt-clad man who just the stepped into the room shattered everything.

"There's only one thing wrong with your story, young man," he said sternly. "You couldn't possibly be from 1952. Time travel has been proved impossible."

Ronald Brisbane let out his breath with a great sigh. He crossed to the window and looked past the roses, out across the landscape, and his sigh changed.

The house stood in the middle of a desert.

"It is desolate, isn't it?" a girl's voice said.

He turned expecting to see still another of the scrawny women of this household. But once again he was surprised. For the girl who stood framed in the archway watching him was one of the most beautiful he had ever seen.

She was slender but softly rounded in all the right places, and there was certainly nothing bony about her legs... Ronald looked back at her face, wondering if he would ever get used to such short tunics.

"I don't think we'll be here much longer," she said. Her voice was low and soft.

Ronald couldn't help staring at her. In any group she would have been lovely but here, contrasted to the others, she was almost unbelievably so. He didn't even notice when the others left the room. He was aware, suddenly, that they were gone.

"Are you one of the family, too?" he asked.

"Yes." She spoke reluctantly, looking down at her feet. "I'm Nora."

"Nora," he said softly. For the first time since he entered this room he stopped regretting having seen this house. "Nora what?"

"Nora Taine," she said. "Didn't anyone introduce you?"

He laughed. "I guess there was too much excitement for formal introductions. I'm Ronald Brisbane. And I really am from 1952."

"I believe you, Ronald." She came over beside him and put her hand on his arm. "Don't mind Father," she said. "He was just awfully upset over the accident."

Her blue tunic matched her eyes perfectly. It clung to her body as she moved, revealing a figure that was young and supple and softly curved. He smiled down at her, wondering how she had ever happened to be born into this family.

"Ronald," she said, "if you're really from that long ago, all this must be very strange to you."

"It is, Nora." He signed. "I wish you'd explain some things to me. In fact, you're the only one I've been really able to talk to."

She flashed him a shy smile. "Thank you," she said.

*   *   *   *   *

She sat down on the couch and he sat down as close beside her as he dared. She glanced over at him, hesitantly. There was something in her manner he couldn't quite figure out. It was almost as though she were afraid of him, and yet she seemed to like him.

"In the first place," he asked, "where are you people from?"

"From? That's rather hard to say. I was born in Africa, while Father was teaching there. So I really am a Terran. Lilian isn't, though she always says she is. She was born on Mars during Father's sabbatical. Mother and Father are Terrans, of course. Only rich people had interplanetary houses then. Junior..."

"No," Ronald said patiently. "That's not what I mean. Where do you live now? When the house isn't moving, that is."

"Oh," Nora smiled. "Up until last semester we lived out at the University of Easter Island. But then Mother wanted more land for an outer garden, so we moved to a new parking lot on one of the artificial islands near the South Pole. It's very well heated."

Ronald repressed a groan. "What year are you from?" he said.

"4823. Your time."

He carefully refrained from asking her what other kinds of timer there were, fearing she would tell him. Instead he said, "I wonder why the English language hasn't changed in all those years?"

"Oh, but it has," Nora said casually. "You wouldn't understand us at all if we talked Terran, and yet that's a direct descendent of English."

"But you're speaking English now. Twentieth-century English. Everyone in your family has been speaking it. And your accents are perfect..."

"Of course," she said. "We're speaking it because you are, to be polite. And naturally we use it correctly. Father has an excellent set of Phonetic Installers. We know all the ancient languages. All educated people do."

"You know all of them?"

"Well, all there are recordings of. Most of the Middle Period Terran languages and High and Low Martian and ..."

"Nora," he said firmly, "about this house of yours. How long have you people had traveling homes?"

"Oh, ever since about—I don't know exactly. I'm not very good at dates. But it's been almost a thousand years."

"And how do these houses work?"

"They're fully automatic. Would you like to see our cooking unit?"

"I would rather see the—er—steering wheel and motor," he said.

She looked at him apologetically. "I don't drive," she said. "If you want anything about the subspace part, you'll have to ask Father. Or Junior. But I guess you won't see Junior tonight. He's been sent to his room."

"Let's talk about something else then," he said.

"Good," Nora said. "What?"

Her blue eyes were sparkling now as they met his and she seemed much less shy. He reached out and took her hand. She didn't draw it away.

"Nora," he said finally, "you're so—so different from the others..."

"Oh!"

She jerked her hand away from his and leaped to her feet, her eyes blazing. "How could you?" she cried. "I thought that you would understand what it was like..."

She turned and ran from the room.

Ronald Brisbane walked slowly to the window and looked out at the encircling desert. The he walked back to the couch and sat down. He was quite sure that he was mad.

*   *   *   *   *

"Oh. There you are young man," Mr. Taine said. This time he had wiped the dirt off his forehead, put a piece of tape over the cut on his cheek and apparently calmed down a little as well.

"Sorry I snapped at you," he said, dropping onto the couch besides Ronald. "But this has been an awfully trying day for me."

"For you?"

Mr. Taine didn't seem to notice the sarcasm. "Yes," he said. "It's my fault, in a way. I should never let Junior drive this morning, not when I had a faculty meeting coming up first period."

He shook his head. "Children have no sense of responsibility these days. Now when I was Junior's age..."

"Please," Ronald said desperately. "All this may seem very natural to you. Wandering around getting your house lost and all that. But it's not what I'm used to. All I want to do is get home again..."

Mr. Taine shrugged. "Well, I'll have the house coils reset in another fifteen minutes," he said. "And I've already patched up the materialize. It wasn't much of an accident, really. Just inconvenient. But I don't see how I can take you into the past, Mr. Brisbane."

Ronald looked at him for a long minute. Then he smiled.

"Perhaps you won't have to," he said.

He got up and walked to the window and gazed out at the desert. It was flat and utterly bleak. It didn't look like any part of Earth he knew, nor even like any of the deserts he had read about. The house might have been on some other planet, except that the sun overhead was definitely Earth's sun.

He turned and looked back at Mr. Taine. "How do you know," he said gently, "that 1952 *is* in the past?"

"Of course it is. History..."

"Look out the window, Mr. Taine. Is your world like that?"

It took a full minute for the implication to sink in. Ronald couldn't help smiling still more at the dismay that seeped slowly into the other's face. Not that it was funny at all, really...

"I thought we were in the Sahara, naturally," Mr. Taine said. "But come to think of it, there should be hydroponics oasis..."

He shook his head and turned away from the window. "No," he said stubbornly. "There's no such thing as time-travel. As soon as the house is ready to go, I'll set it for Easter Island and take you with us to the University. They may be able to help you there."

*   *   *   *   *

"Well," Mr. Taine said half an hour later. "We're almost there."

He and Ronald were standing in the control room, looking out through the glass walls at the black nothingness of sub-space that enfolded the garden. Behind them, in the master bedroom, Lilian and her mother crowded against the control room door, waiting.

Ronald couldn't see Nora, although he knew she was there. She had taken a seat on the far side of the bedroom, out of sight of the controls. And she wouldn't even speak to him.

"All we have to do now is warp back up," Mr. Taine was saying. "You see, private houses have to travel slowly, in their own assigned lanes, and it's the crossing into and out of sub-space that takes time. Traffic jams."

The red light over the dial was marked with the symbol that Mr. Taine had translated as Sub-Space Warpage; it was blinking slower and slower, and the calibrated dial read almost zero. Mr. Taine moved the rudder into neutral.

"That should do it," he remarked cheerfully.

The house slowed to a stop, gently this time. The blackness gradually seeped away, replaced by blue sky and a blue ocean, and about thirty feet directly underneath them, a barren, rocky island. The paused, Mr. Taine making no effort to land the house, and looked down through the transparent floor viewer.

"Well," Mr. Taine sighed. "You were right."

"Father," Lilian called. "What's the matter? Where are the buildings?"

Mr. Taine and Ronald looked at each other helplessly. Then the older man sighed again. "We'll have to tell them," he said.

They went out into the bedroom. Lilian and her mother leaned forward eagerly.

"Why is it taking us so long?" Lilian asked.

"Your books are wrong," he said gently. "There really is time travel. And we're in the past somewhere—the far past."

"Oh, how exciting!"

The Lilian's squeal changed midway into a squawk of terror. "But how are we going to get home?"

"Yes," her mother said. "Exploring the past may be all right for you men, but I have a club meeting this afternoon..."

Ronald Brisbane put his hands in his pockets and strode quickly out of the room. He crossed over to what was apparently a glassed-in observation veranda and sat down on the swing chair and tried to think.

A few minutes later he jumped up again.

"Junior!" he exclaimed. "Of course!"

It was all very simple, suddenly. All he had to do was find Junior and ask him what he had done to the drive mechanism of the house. Because it was obvious that Junior had done something to it.

"Nora!" he called. "Will you come here a minute?"

There was quick silence, then the sound of footsteps, muffled against the soft carpeting.

"What is it, Ronald?" she asked.

For a minute, watching her, Ronald forgot all about Junior and the problem of the house. He could only stare at her admiringly.

She smiled at him. "You called me," she said.

"Yes, I did." He forced his thoughts away from her. "Where is Junior, Nora? I want to talk to him."

Nora frowned. "I don't know if Father would like that. He's in his room being punished for..."

"For wrecking the house. I know that. But I still want to see him, and it's important. Maybe he can unwreck it again. Which room is his, Nora?"

"Right down the hall." She glanced back toward her parents' room, but no one was looking out. "Here, I'll show you," she said.

*   *   *   *   *

He followed her down the hall to a small curtained archway. As they stepped through it, Ronald found himself wondering what Junior would be like. Probably a normal, prank-playing youngster, though if he looked like his father..."

"Ouch!" Ronald yelled as something hot and tingling slashed across his ankles. He stumbled forward across the room.

Blue fire ate up his legs to his knees, then burned out abruptly. With its cessation, there came a sudden thump, a gasp, and the figure of a boy falling apparently from the ceiling and landing about six inches from Ronald's feet. The boy rolled over, sat up, and glared.

"What..." Ronald began, rubbing an ankle that felt as if it had just come out of an oven.

Junior interrupted him. "Did you really *have* to step in my Throndike field?" he said. "You could hurt a guy that way."

Ronald limped over to Junior's bed and sat down. "I realize that," he said.

He eyed Junior warily, quite certain now that he had found the person responsible for marooning them somewhere. Junior would undoubtedly be capable of anything. Ronald flexed his toes, wincing a little as the stiffness left them.

"All right, Junior," he said. "You might as well tell me. What did you do to the sub-space drive that made the house come here?"

The boy stood up an rearranged his orange plaid kilts. The he smiled at Ronald, the blankly innocent look of a medieval cherub superimposed upon his thin, ugly face.

"Do?" he said. "Why I didn't even *touch* the drive. Is something wrong?"

His smile grew even broader as Ronald and Nora looked helplessly at each other.

"Please, Junior," Nora said for the twentieth time. "Tell us what you did to the controls. You must have done something..."

Junior shook his head again. "But I didn't Nora," he protested. "You know that Dad made me promise to never fool around with the drive mechanism."

He picked up another coil of wire and added it to the complicated pyramidal structure he was assembling on the rug. Then he bent forward, studying it. The knowledge that they were where they had been a few hours previously didn't seem to interest him in the least.

"But Junior..." Nora said.

"I don't break my promises," Junior sniffed. "If I did, do you think Dad would ever let me drive again? Or even take the annex out on Sundays? You know how he is about things like that."

Nora turned helplessly to Ronald. "If he does know anything," she said, "he's not going to tell us."

Ronald thought back over all the child psychology he had ever read about. He wished now that he had paid a little more attention to the subject.

Junior connected another strand of wire and sat back on his heels and grinned at his work. "Nice job, isn't it?" he said. "Now I'll just start her up..."

He floated casually back up to the ceiling. "Be careful you don't step in the field again when you go out," he called down.

Ronald glared up at where the boy lay stretched out comfortably in the empty air, well out of reach. Then he forced a pleasant smile onto his face.

"Junior," he said. "Why don't you tell me what you did to the house? I won't let your father know, I promise. Then I can go and change it back and ..."

"Huh," Junior drew his knees up under his chin and hugged them. "Why should I tell *you* anything? I don't even like you."

"Junior!" Nora snapped. "He's our guest."

"Some guest. Trying to order us all around."

Junior stretched out full length once more and closed his eyes.

Ronald opened his mouth to speak, realized that what he was going to say wasn't the sort of language he would want Nora to hear and closed it again. Finally he turned to the girl.

"Go get your father," he said.

"But he'll be angry."

"Not at you."   Then, as she still hesitated, he added. "Oh, all right. I'll go with you."

She started toward the archway, stepping carefully and apparently automatically over the Throndike field, and Ronald followed her.

"It won't do you any good," Junior said from above their heads.

Ronald didn't answer.

"And you're too dumb to figure it out yourself," Junior added.

Ronald paused, his hand already on the archway curtain. He looked up at Junior, who had now rolled over on his stomach and lay grinning down at them. The grin was too much.

Very deliberately Ronald drew back his left foot and kicked into the Throndike field. The fire that shot up his leg was agonizing, but he smiled despite it. It was well worth a second's pain to see the grin vanish from Junior's face as catapulted to the floor.

"We'll be right back, Junior," he said.   Then he limped out into the hall after Nora.

*   *   *   *   *

Mr. Taine glanced questioningly at his son, then back at Ronald. "What's this about Junior now?" he asked.

"Nothing," Ronald said. "Except that he must have done something to the drive that made it bring us here. That's all."

Mr. Taine blinked. Then he shook his head. "Oh, no, I'm sure he wouldn't do anything like that."   He paused, then added, "You didn't, did you, Junior?"

"Of course not, Father."

Mr. Taine spread his hands and smiled. "You see," he said. "He didn't do it."

Ronald groaned. "I suppose this house just came here all by itself," he said.   "Across all those thousands of years..."

Mr. Taine smiled apologetically. "I know that you're anxious to get home, young man," he said. "So am I. But I'm sure there's a more logical explanation to all this. Time travel..."

"Has been proved impossible," Ronald finished the sentence for him. "I know. It's too bad, though," he added. "Just think what it would mean if someone figured out how to make time travel really work."

"It can't be done," Mr. Taine said. "There's only one way that a sub-space field can flow. Parallel to normal time. That's in all the books. Though you wouldn't have read them, naturally."

"So there's no way of changing the flow," Ronald said. "What a pity. It would make an interesting experiment..."

"Of course, of course," Mr. Taine said. But it just can't be done.

Ronald looked straight at Junior as he said softly, "No, I suppose you're right." His face was turned so that only the boy could see him wink.

Junior shot him a startled glance, then suddenly grinned back. His look of suspicion faded, replaced by a certain grudging admiration.

"You know, Dad," he said, "I've been thinking."

Junior stood up, stretched, and then crossed the room to where the Throndike field apparatus lay dismantled on the floor. He bent down, picked up the pieces, put them away in a box, locked it and pocketed the key. The he straightened up again and started for the archway.

"It's a pretty good idea, too," he said. "I bet that flow could be changed. If you set up a cross-current in the sub-space elements..."

Mr. Taine, after his first startled headshake, smiled down at his son. "Do you really think so, Junior?"

The son shrugged. "How should I know? I never tried it."

Ronald snorted under his breath.

"But I could take a look," Junior said. "If you let me go back in the control room and drive, that is."

Mr. Taine hesitated a moment, frowning. Then he nodded.

"I guess you've been punished enough," he said. "After all, you were just being careless when you crashed us. And if you think you can get us home..."

*   *   *   *   *

"There," Junior said, hooking the second wire securely in place. "Now I'll start her up and see where we go."

The blackness came quickly. The dial blinked red, faster and faster, then steadied off for perhaps half a minute.   Junior flicked the switch and the blinking slowed.

There was a slight bump as the house landed. "Look out and see where we are," Junior said. "I may not have the space and time coordinated right.   Sub-sub's awfully tricky..."

The blackness had thinned into a murky, greenish twilight.   They sat waiting for it to thin more, but it didn't.   Outside everything was a strange, light filled translucence.

"Good heavens," Nora muttered. "When is this?"

Just then Lilian screamed. "Look out there!"

They turned to where she was pointing, just as she fainted. For once Ronald didn't blame her. The gigantic shark-like fish looking in at them was enough to make anyone faint.

"Get us out of here," Ronald ordered.

Junior didn't need any urging. He flicked them back into sub-space and the blackness flowed around them again.

"Go the other way, Junior," Ronald suggested. "We're probably still traveling back into the past."

"How do you figure that?"

"Because we're moving through time, not space. And we were just at a time when the ocean was higher and there wasn't any Easter Island."

The boy flicked one of the dials. "All right," he said. "We'll try it."

"We've got a long way to go yet," Ronald said. "This drive must be really powerful."

"Sure," Junior admitted. "I souped it up some."

A few moments passed.

"I can calibrate us in from here," Junior said suddenly. "I'm picking up the University signal in sub-sub."

Once again the dials zeroed and the blackness thinned.

"Where are we?" Mrs. Taine crowded towards the window.

"Home," Junior grunted. "Look over there."

"The University?"

They pressed up against the window, making excited, happy sounds. A moment later Mr. Taine pressed a button that opened the control room window and leaned out. The man in the central tower casually waved at him.

"Oh, hello there," he said. "You're late this morning. Your class went over to Asia without you. Mr. Ricard substituted."

Mr. Taine smiled, "Thanks, Charlie," he said. He closed the window. "Well, he said, "we're home, Junior, you've done a great job. I'm really proud of you, son,"

Junior grinned. His father clapped him heartily on the shoulder. "So time travel's really possible," he said.

Lilian had stopped crying. Now she was busily rubbing her eyelids with purple mascara. "I look a sight," she muttered.

"You sure do," Ronald said under his breath.

Nora giggled, and he realized that he must have spoken louder than he had intended. He smiled down at her.

She looked up at him, her eyes shining. She had forgotten all about being shy, or angry, or upset, and now she was just beautiful.

"You're wonderful, Nora," he said.

"Do you really think so, Ronald?"

Outside the house was a civilization almost three thousand years in the future, with all the wonders that man would dream up during those years; but Ronald didn't even glance towards the window. He was looking, right now, at the most marvelous woman in any age...

"Say, young man," Mr. Taine interrupted. "I forgot about you. I'll have to see about sending you home."

Ronald looked up slowly. "Yes," he sighed. "Though I could stay here..."

Mr. Taine's smile froze. Mrs. Taine gasped, and even Lilian stared at him in dismay. Nora squeezed his arm.

"What's the matter?" Ronald said. "Have I said something wrong? Why can't I stay her if I want to?"

"Ronald," Nora said softly. "Don't you know?"

"Know what?"

Then she laughed, gayly, with a light in her eyes that he hadn't seen there before. "So it's different in your time," she said. "I should have guessed it."

The others were still staring at him, and he realized suddenly that their look was mostly one of pity. Even Lilian was pitying him.

Nora took his hand and held it tightly. "Look at them," she said. "Mother, Father, Junior, Lilian."

He looked at them. They no longer seemed so strange, so outlandish, though they were thin and gawky and altogether the homeliest family he had ever seen. But of course he was used to this by now...

"They're normal," Nora said. "And we're freaks. Both of us, though I'm more of one than you, actually."

*   *   *   *   *

"Look," the real-estate agent said. "I'm telling you what I saw. He went into the house..."

"The house that wasn't there. I know, I know." The policeman shook his head. "You better go on home for a while."

"But it's just around the corner. You've got to believe me, officer."

"Sure, I believe you. A house came down on a vacant lot and your client went in and it flew away with him. You better go on home and rest for awhile."

The real-estate agent mopped his forehead. He realized now that he had been foolish, telling the policeman. It wasn't the sort of story that anyone would believe. In fact, he didn't even believe it himself, exactly, any more.

They turned the corner and started towards the end of the subdivision. Ahead of them were four Plan B type houses on one side of the street and the vacant lot on the other. The agent sighed. It was, after all, a very hot day.

"Well," said the policeman, "you were right about the house being there, anyway. Funny, I don't remember anyone getting a permit to bring one in along the street."

The agent looked up slowly. He knew even before he saw it that it would be a Moorish type house with a well-tended garden. It was.

"I'll have to check on this," the policeman said.

The door of the house opened and tow people came out. The real-estate agent swallowed. One was definitely the young man—Brisbane—who had vanished along with the house. The other was a girl in a very brief dress...

"Oh, hello there," Ronald Brisbane called out. "You're just the man I want—"

The agent backed off a couple of steps, then remembered that there was a policeman along. "Yes?" he said.

"I want to buy a house," Ronald Brisbane said.

"That one? I don't..."

Ronald frowned, "No, not that one."

"Say, lady," the policeman said. "Don't you know there's a city ordinance against—well, against—I mean, don't you know that..."

He turned a bit redder and looked up, with an effort, at Nora's face. She smiled.

"She's my wife," Ronald said belligerently. "We were just married and I haven't had time to buy her any clothes."

The agent groaned. Ronald glanced back at him. "Oh, yes, the house," he said. "No, I want one of those."

He strode across the street, with Nora right behind him. He crossed the sidewalk in front of House 22, went up the flagstone walk and paused at the door.

"We'll take this one," he said. "And where's the justice of the peace? I think we'd better get married again. I don't know if ours is legal now."

The agent looked over at the policeman, but his attention was fastened on Nora's tunic.

"I thought you didn't like these houses," the agent said weakly.

"I like them now," Ronald said fervently. "Don't you, darling?"

She smiled up at him. "Oh, yes," she whispered. "I love this house, Ronald."

The real-estate agent choked suddenly. When he looked up again, Ronald Brisbane was just carrying his bride across the threshold.

"Love," the policeman said. "It's a wonderful thing, isn't it?" He shrugged. "So there's a house brought in without a permit. So what? I'm not going to bother them about it." He walked off.

The agent stood on the lawn of House 22 and watched until the policeman was almost to the corner. Then, slowly and with great determination, he strode across the street and up the path through the rose garden. He was going to find out, once and for all, whether or not the house was real.

Once he looked back towards the policeman, but he had already turned the corner. The agent shrugged and tried the door handle. It wasn't locked. He took a deep breath, noticing how particularly sweet this kind of roses smelled, and pulled the door open.

Ronald and Nora paused just inside the doorway of their new, quite ordinary, absolutely stationary, and wholly desirable house. After they had kissed and kissed again, Nora drew away.

"I want to wave goodbye to the family," she said.

They went to the window. Ronald smiled ruefully. "We're too late," he said. Across the street was nothing but a vacant lot.

HOMO INFERIOR

ILLUSTRATED BY RUDOLPH PALAIS
ORIGINALLY PUBLISHED IN *IF WORLDS OF SCIENCE FICTION*
NOVEMBER 1953

Homo Inferior

The starship waited. Cylindrical walls enclosed it, and a transparent plastic dome held it back from the sky and the stars. It waited, while night changed to day and back again, while the seasons merged one into another, and the years, and the centuries. It towered as gleaming and as uncorroded as it had when it was first built, long ago, when men had bustled about it and in it, their shouting and their laughter and the sound of their tools ringing against the metallic plates.

Now few men ever came to it. And those who did come merely looked with quiet faces for a few minutes, and then went away again.

The generations kaleidoscoped by. The Starship waited.

*　　*　　*　　*　　*

Eric met the other children when he was four years old. They were out in the country, and he'd slipped away from his parents and started wading along the edge of a tiny stream, kicking at the water spiders.

His feet were soaked, and his knees were streaked with mud where he'd knelt down to play. His father wouldn't like it later, but right now it didn't matter. It was fun to be off by himself, splashing along the stream, feeling the sun hot on his back and the water icy against his feet.

A water spider scooted past him, heading for the tangled moss along the bank. He bent down, scooped his hand through the water to catch it. For a moment he had it, then it slipped over his fingers and darted away, out of his reach.

As he stood up, disappointed, he saw them: two boys and a girl, not much older than he. They were standing at the edge of the trees, watching him.

He'd seen children before, but he'd never met any of them. His parents kept him away from them—and from all strangers. He stood still, watching them, waiting for them to say something. He felt excited and uncomfortable at the same time.

They didn't say anything. They just watched him, very intently.

He felt even more uncomfortable.

The bigger boy laughed. He pointed at Eric and laughed again and looked over at his companions. They shook their heads.

Eric waded up out of the water. He didn't know whether to go over to them or run away, back to his mother. He didn't understand the way they were looking at him.

"Hello," he said.

The big boy laughed again. "See?" he said, pointing at Eric. "He can't."

"Can't what?" Eric said.

The three looked at him, not saying anything. Then they all burst out laughing. They pointed at him, jumped up and down and clapped their hands together.

"What's funny?" Eric said, backing away from them, wishing his mother would come, and yet afraid to turn around and run.

"You," the girl said. "You're funny. Funny, funny, funny! You're stu-pid."

The others took it up. "Stu-pid, stu-pid. You can't talk to us, you're too stu-pid...."

They skipped down the bank toward him, laughing and calling. They jumped up and down and pointed at him, crowded closer and closer.

"Silly, silly. Can't talk. Silly, silly. Can't talk...."

Eric backed away from them. He tried to run, but he couldn't. His knees shook too much. He could hardly move his legs at all. He began to cry.

They crowded still closer around him. "Stu-pid." Their laughter was terrible. He couldn't get away from them. He cried louder.

"Eric!" His mother's voice. He twisted around, saw her coming, running toward him along the bank.

"Mama!" He could move again. He stumbled toward her.

"He wants his mama," the big boy said. "Funny baby."

His mother was looking past him, at the other children. They stopped laughing abruptly. They looked back at her for a moment, scuffing their feet in the dirt and not saying anything. Suddenly the big boy turned and ran, up over the bank and out of sight. The other boy followed him.

The girl started to run, and then she looked at Eric's mother again and stopped. She looked back at Eric. "I'm sorry," she said sulkily, and then she turned and fled after the others.

Eric's mother picked him up. "It's all right," she said. "Mother's here. It's all right."

He clung to her, clutching her convulsively, his whole body shaking. "Why, Mama? Why?"

"You're all right, dear."

She was warm and her arms were tight around him. He was home again, and safe. He relaxed, slowly.

"Don't leave me, Mama."

"I won't, dear."

She crooned to him, softly, and he relaxed still more. His head drooped on her shoulder and after a while he fell asleep.

But it wasn't the same as it had been. It wouldn't ever be quite the same again. He knew he was different now.

*   *   *   *   *

That night Eric lay asleep. He was curled on his side, one chubby hand under his cheek, the other still holding his favorite animal, the wooly lamb his mother had given him for his birthday. He stirred in his sleep, threshing restlessly, and whimpered.

His mother's face lifted mutely to her husband's.

"Myron, the things those children said. It must have been terrible for him. I'm glad at least that he couldn't perceive what they were thinking."

Myron sighed. He put his arm about her shoulders and drew her close against him. "Don't torture yourself, Gwin. You can't make it easier for him. There's no way."

"But we'll have to tell him something."

He stroked her hair. The four years of their shared sorrow lay heavily between them as he looked down over her head at his son.

"Poor devil. Let him keep his childhood while he can, Gwin. He'll know he's all alone soon enough."

She nodded, burying her face against his chest. "I know...."

Eric whimpered again, and his hands clenched into fists and came up to protect his face.

Instinctively Gwin reached out to him, and then she drew back. She couldn't reach his emotions. There was no perception. There was no way she could enter his dreams and rearrange them and comfort him.

"Poor devil," his father said again. "He's got his whole life to be lonely in."

                    *   *   *   *   *

The summer passed, and another winter and another summer. Eric spent more and more time by himself. He liked to sit on the glassed-in sunporch, bouncing his ball up and down and talking to it, aloud, pretending that it answered him back. He liked to lie on his stomach close to the wall and look out at the garden with its riotous mass of flowers and the insects that flew among them. Some flew quickly, their wings moving so fast that they were just blurs. Others flew slowly, swooping on outspread bright-colored wings from petal to petal. He liked these slow-flying ones the best. He could wiggle his shoulder blades in time with their wings and pretend that he was flying too.

Sometimes other children came by on the outside of the wall. He could look out at them without worrying, because they couldn't see him. The wall wasn't transparent from the outside. He liked it when three or four of them came by together, laughing and chasing each other through the garden. Usually, though, they didn't stay long. After they had played a few minutes his father or his mother went out and looked at them, and then they went away.

Eric was playing by himself when the old man came out to the sunporch doorway and stood there, saying nothing, making no effort to interrupt or to speak. He was so quiet that after a while Eric almost didn't mind his being there.

The old man turned back to Myron and Gwin.

"Of course the boy can learn. He's not stupid."

Eric bounced the ball, flung it against the transparent glass, caught it, bounced it again.

"But how, Walden?" Gwin shook her head. "You offer to teach him, but—"

Walden smiled. "Remember *these?*"

... Walden's study. The familiar curtains drawn aside, and the shelves behind them. The rows of bright-backed, box-like objects, most of them old and spotted, quite unhygienic ...

Gwin shook her head at the perception, but Myron nodded.

"Books. I didn't know there were any outside the museums."

Walden smiled again. "Only mine. Books are fascinating things. All the knowledge of a race, gathered together on a few shelves...."

"Knowledge?" Myron shrugged. "Imagine storing knowledge in those—boxes. What are they? What's in them? Just words...."

The books faded as Walden sighed. "You'd be surprised what the old race did, with just those—boxes."

He looked across at Eric, who was now bouncing his ball and counting, out loud, up to three, and then going back and starting again.

"The boy can learn what's in those books. Just as if he'd gone to school back in the old times."

Myron and Gwin looked doubtfully at each other, and then over at the corner where Eric played unheeding. Perhaps Walden could help. Perhaps....

"Eric," Gwin said aloud.

"Yes, mother?"

"We've decided you're going to go to school, the way you want to. Mr. Walden here is going to be your teacher. Isn't that nice?"

Eric looked at her and then at the old man. Strangers didn't often come out on the sunporch. Strangers usually left him alone.

He bounced the ball again without answering.

"Say something, Eric," his mother commanded.

Eric looked back at Walden. "He can't teach me to be like other children, can he?"

"No," Walden said. "I can't."

"Then I don't want to go to school." Eric threw the ball across the room as hard as he could.

"But there once were other people like *you*," Walden said. "Lots of them. And you can learn about them, if you want to."

"Other people like me? Where?"

Myron and Gwin looked helplessly at each other and at the old man. Gwin began to cry and Myron cursed softly, on the perception level so that Eric wouldn't hear them.

But Walden's face was gentle and understanding as he answered, so understanding that Eric couldn't help wanting desperately to believe him.

"Everyone was like you once," Walden said. "A long time ago."

*   *   *   *   *

It was a new life for Eric. Every day he would go over to Walden's and the two of them would pull back the curtains in the study and Walden would lift down some of the books. It was as if Walden was giving him the past, all of it, as fast as he could grasp it.

"I'm really like the old race, Walden?"

"Yes, Eric. You'll see just how much like them...."

Identity. Here in the past, in the books he was learning to read, in the pictures, the pages and pages of scenes and portraits. Strange scenes, far removed from the gardens and the quiet houses and the wordless smile of friend to friend.

Great buildings and small. The Parthenon in the moonlight, not too many pages beyond the cave, with its smoky fire and first crude wall drawings. Cities bright with a million neon lights, and still later, caves again— the underground stations of the Moon colonies. All unreal, and yet—

They were his people, these men in the pictures. Strange men, violent men: the barbarian trampling his enemy to death beneath his horse's hooves, the knight in armor marching to the Crusade, the spaceman. And the quieter men: the farmer, the artisan, the poet—they too were his people, and far easier to understand than the others.

The skill of reading mastered, and the long, sweeping vistas of the past. Their histories. Their wars. "Why did they fight, Walden?" And Walden's sigh. "I don't know, Eric, but they did."

So much to learn. So much to understand. Their art and music and literature and religion. Patterns of life that ebbed and flowed and ebbed again, but never in quite the same way. "Why did they change so much, Walden?" And the answer, "You probably know that better than I, Eric...."

Perhaps he did. For he went on to the books that Walden ignored. Their mathematics, their science. The apple's fall, and the orbits of planets. The sudden spiral of analysis, theory, technology. The machines—steamships, airplanes, spaceships....

And the searching loneliness that carried the old race from the caves of Earth to the stars. The searching, common to the violent man and the quiet man, to the doer and the dreaming poet.

Why do we hunger, who own the Moon and trample the shifting dust   of Mars?

Why aren't we content with the worlds we've won? Why don't we   rest, with the system ours?

We have cast off the planets like outgrown toys, and now we want   the stars....

"Have you ever been to the stars, Walden?"

Walden stared at him. Then he laughed. "Of course not, Eric. Nobody goes there now. None of our race has ever gone. Why should we?"

There was no explaining. Walden had never been lonely.

And then one day, while he was reading some fiction from the middle period of the race, Eric found the fantasy. Speculation about the future, about their future.... About the new race!

He read on, his heart pounding, until the same old pattern came clear. They had foreseen conflict, struggle between old race and new, suspicion and hatred and tragedy. The happy ending was superficial. Everyone was motivated as they had been motivated.

He shut the book and sat there, wanting to reach back across the years to the old race writers who had been so right and yet so terribly, blindly wrong. The writers who had seen in the new only a continuation of the old, of themselves, of their own fears and their own hungers.

"Why did they die, Walden?" He didn't expect an answer.

"Why does any race die, Eric?"

His own people, forever removed from him, linked to him only through the books, the pictures, and his own backward-reaching emotions.

"Walden, hasn't there *ever* been anyone else like me, since they died?"

Silence. Then, slowly, Walden nodded.

"I wondered how long it would be before you asked that. Yes, there have been others. Sometimes three or four in a generation."

"Then, perhaps...."

"No," Walden said. "There aren't any others now. We'd know it if there were." He turned away from Eric, to the plastic wall that looked out across the garden and the children playing and the long, level, flower-carpeted plain.

"Sometimes, when there's more than one of them, they go out there away from us, out to the hills where it's wild. But they're found, of course. Found, and brought back." He sighed. "The last of them died when I was a boy."

Others like him. Within Walden's lifetime, others, cut off from their own race, lonely and rootless in the midst of the new. Others like him, but not now, in his lifetime. For him there were only the books.

The old race was gone, gone with all its conflicts, all its violence, its stupidity—and its flaming rockets in the void and its Parthenon in the moonlight.

*   *   *   *   *

Eric came into the study and stopped. The room was filled with strangers. There were half a dozen men besides Walden, most of them fairly old, white-haired and studious looking. They all turned to look at him, watched him gravely without speaking.

"Well, there he is." Walden looked from face to face. "Are you still worried? Do you still think that one small boy constitutes a threat to the race? What about you, Abbot?"

"I don't know. I still think he should have been institutionalized in the beginning."

"Why? So you could study the brain processes of the lower animals?" Walden's thoughts were as sarcastic as he could send them.

"No, of course not. But don't you see what you've done, by teaching him to read? You've started him thinking of the old race. Don't deny it."

"I don't."

The thin man, Drew, broke in angrily. "He's not full grown yet. Just fourteen, isn't he? How can you be sure what he'll be like later? He'll be a problem. They've always been problems."

They were afraid. That was what was the matter with them. Walden sighed. "Tell them what you've been studying, Eric," he said aloud.

For a minute Eric was too tongue-tied to answer. He stood motionless, waiting for them to laugh at him.

"Go on. Tell them."

"I've been reading about the old race," Eric said. "All about the stars. About the people who went off in the starships and explored our whole galaxy."

"What's a galaxy?" the thin man said. Walden could perceive that he really didn't know.

Eric's fear lessened. These men weren't laughing at him. They weren't being just polite, either. They were interested. He smiled at them, shyly, and told them about the books and the wonderful, strange tales of the past that the books told. The men listened, nodding from time to time. But he knew that they didn't understand. The world of the books was his alone....

"Well?" Walden looked at the others. They looked back. Their emotions were a welter of doubt, of indecision.

"You've heard the boy," Walden said quietly, thrusting his own uneasiness down, out of his thoughts.

"Yes." Abbot hesitated. "He seems bright enough—quite different from what I'd expected. At least he's not like the ones who grew up wild in the hills. This boy isn't a savage."

Walden shrugged. "Maybe they weren't savages either," he suggested. "After all, it's been fifty years since the last of them died. And a lot of legends can spring up in fifty years."

"Perhaps we have been worrying unnecessarily." Abbot got up to go, but his eyes still held Walden's. "But," he added, "it's up to you to watch him. If he reverts, becomes dangerous in any way, he'll have to be locked up. That's final."

The others nodded.

"I'll watch him," Walden told them. "Just stop worrying."

He stood at the door and waited until they were out of sight. Then and only then did he allow himself to sigh and taste the fear he'd kept hidden. The old men, the men with authority, were the dangerous ones.

Walden snorted. Even with perception, men could be fools.

*   *   *   *   *

The summer that Eric was sixteen Walden took him to the museum. The aircar made the trip in just a few hours—but it was farther than Eric had ever traveled in his life, and farther than most people ever bothered traveling.

The museum lay on an open plain where there weren't many houses. At first glance it was far from impressive. Just a few big buildings, housing the artifacts, and a few old ruins of ancient constructions, leveled now and half buried in the sands.

"It's nothing." Eric looked down at it, disappointed. "Nothing at all."

"What did you expect?" Walden set the aircar down between the two largest buildings. "You knew it wouldn't be like the pictures in the books. You knew that none of the old race's cities are left."

"I know," Eric said. "But I expected more than this."

He got out of the car and followed Walden around to the door of the first building. Another man, almost as old as Walden, came toward them smiling. The two men shook hands and stood happily perceiving each other.

"This is Eric," Walden said aloud. "Eric, this is Prior, the caretaker here. He was one of my schoolmates."

"It's been years since we've perceived short range," Prior said. "Years. But I suppose the boy wants to look around inside?"

Eric nodded, although he didn't care too much. He was too disappointed to care. There was nothing here that he hadn't seen a hundred times before.

They went inside, past some scale models of the old cities. The same models, though a bit bigger, that Eric had seen in the three-dimensional view-books. Then they went into another room, lined with thousands of books, some very old, many the tiny microfilmed ones from the middle periods of the old race.

"How do you like it, Eric?" the caretaker said.

"It's fine," he said flatly, not really meaning it. He was angry at himself for feeling disappointment. Walden had told him what to expect. And yet he'd kept thinking that he'd walk into one of the old cities and be able to imagine that it was ten thousand years ago and others were around him. Others like him....

Ruins. Ruins covered by dirt, and no one of the present race would even bother about uncovering them.

Prior and Walden looked at each other and smiled. "Did you tell him?" the caretaker telepathed.

"No. I thought we'd surprise him. I knew all the rest would disappoint him."

"Eric," the caretaker said aloud. "Come this way. There's another room I want to show you."

He followed them downstairs, down a long winding ramp that spiraled underground so far that he lost track of the distance they had descended. He didn't much care anyway. Ahead of him, the other two were communicating, leaving him alone.

"Through here," Prior said, stepping off the ramp.

They entered a room that was like the bottom of a well, with smooth stone sides and far, far above them a glass roof, with clouds apparently drifting across its surface. But it wasn't a well. It was a vault, forever preserving the thing that had been the old race's masterpiece.

It rested in the center of the room, its nose pointing up at the sky. It was like the pictures, and unlike them. It was big, far bigger than Eric had ever visualized it. It was tall and smooth and as new looking as if its builders had just stepped outside for a minute and would be back in another minute to blast off for the stars.

"A starship," Walden said. "One of the last types."

"There aren't many left," Prior said. "We're lucky to have this one in our museum."

Eric wasn't listening. He was looking at the ship. The old race's ship. His ship.

"The old race built strange things," Prior said. "This is one of the strangest." He shook his head. "Imagine the time they put in on it.... And for what?"

Eric didn't try to answer him. He couldn't explain why the old ones had built it. But he knew. He would have built it himself, if he'd lived then. *We have cast off the planets like outgrown toys, and now we want the stars....*

His people. His ship. His dream.

* * * * *

The old caretaker showed him around the museum and then left him alone to explore by himself. He had all the time he wanted.

He studied. He worked hard all day long, scarcely ever leaving the museum grounds. He studied the subjects that now were the most fascinating to him of all the old race's knowledge—the subjects that related to the starships. Astronomy, physics, navigation, and the complex charts of distant stars, distant planets, worlds he'd never heard of before. Worlds that to the new race were only pin-pricks of light in the night sky.

All day long he studied. But in the evening he would go down the winding ramp to the ship. The well was lighted with a softer, more diffuse illumination than that of the houses. In the soft glow the walls and the glass-domed roof seemed to disappear and the ship looked free, pointing up at the stars.

He didn't try to tell the caretaker what he thought. He just went back to his books and his studies. There was so much he had to learn. And now there was a reason for his learning. Someday, when he was fully grown and strong and had mastered all he needed from the books, he was going to fly the ship. He was going to look for his people, the ones who had left Earth before the new race came....

He told no one. But Walden watched him, and sighed.

"They'll never let you do it, Eric. It's a mad dream."

"What are you talking about?"

"The ship. You want to go to the stars, don't you?"

Eric stared at him, more surprised than he'd been in years. He had said nothing. There was no way for Walden to know. Unless he'd perceived it—and Eric couldn't be perceived, any more than he could perceive other people....

Walden shook his head. "It wasn't telepathy that told me. It was your eyes. The way you look at the ship. And besides, I've known you for years now. And I've wondered how long it would be before you thought of this answer."

"Well, why not?" Eric looked across at the ship, and his throat caught, choking him, the way it always did. "I'm lonely here. My people are gone. Why shouldn't I go?"

"You'd be lonelier inside that ship, by yourself, away from Earth, away from everything, and with no assurance you'd ever find anyone at all, old race or new or alien...."

Eric didn't answer. He looked back at the ship, thinking of the books, trying to think of it as a prison, a weightless prison carrying him forever into the unknown, with no one to talk to, no one to see.

Walden was right. He would be too much alone in the ship. He'd have to postpone his dream.

He'd wait until he was old, and take the ship and die in it....

Eric smiled at the thought. He was seventeen, old enough to know that his idea was adolescent and melodramatic. He knew, suddenly, that he'd never fly the ship.

*   *   *   *   *

The years passed. Eric spent most of his time at the museum. He had his own aircar now, and sometimes he flew it home and visited with his parents. They liked to have him come. They liked it much better than having to travel all the way to the museum to visit him.

Yet, though he wasn't dependent on other people any more, and could fly the aircar as he chose, he didn't do much exploring. He didn't have any desire to meet strangers. And there were always the books.

"You're sure you're all right?" his mother said. "You don't need anything?"

"No. I'm fine."

He smiled, looking out through the sunporch wall into the garden. It seemed years and years since he'd pressed his nose to the glass, watching the butterflies. It had been a long time.

"I've got to get going," he said. "I want to be back at the museum by dark."

"Well, if you're sure you won't stay...."

They said goodbye and he went out and got into the aircar and started back. He flew slowly, close to the ground, because he really had plenty of time and he felt lazy. He skimmed along over a valley and heard laughter and dipped lower. A group of children was playing. Young ones—they even talked aloud sometimes as they played. Children.... There were so many children, always in groups, laughing....

He flew on, quickly, until he was in a part of the country where he didn't see any houses. Just a stream and a grove of trees and bright flowers. He dropped lower, stopped, got out and walked down to the stream.

It was by another stream that he'd met the children who had laughed at him, years ago. He smiled, sadly.

He felt alone, but in a different sense from his usual isolation. He felt free, away from people, away even from the books and their unspoken insistence that their writers were dead and almost forgotten. He stood by the edge of the stream, watching water spiders scoot across the rippled surface.

This was the same. This stream had probably been here when the old race was here, maybe even before the old race had even come into existence.

Water spiders. Compared to man, their race was immortal....

The sun was low when he turned away from the stream and walked back to where he had parked the aircar. He scarcely looked about him as he walked. He was sure he was alone, and he felt no caution, no need to watch and listen.

But as he turned toward the car he saw the people. Two. Young, about his own age. A boy and a girl, smiling at each other, holding hands.

They weren't a dozen feet in front of him. But they didn't notice him. They were conscious of no one but each other. As Eric watched, standing frozen, unwilling to draw attention to himself by even moving or backing up, the two leaned closer together. Their arms went around each other, tightly, and they kissed.

They said nothing. They kissed, and then stood apart and went on looking at each other. Even without being able to perceive, Eric could feel their emotion.

Then they turned, slowly, toward him. In a moment they would be aware of him. He didn't want them to think he was spying on them, so he went toward them, making no effort to be quiet, and as he moved they stepped still farther apart and looked at him, startled.

They looked at each other as he passed, even more startled, and the girl's hand went up to her mouth in surprise.

They know, Eric thought bitterly. They know I'm different.

He didn't want to go back to the museum. He flew blindly, not looking down at the neat domed houses and the gardens and the people, but ahead, to the eastern sky and the upthrust scarp of the hills. The hills, where people like him had fled, for a little while.

The occasional aircars disappeared. The gardens dropped away, and the ordered color, and there was grass and bare dirt and, ahead, the scraggly trees and out-thrust rocks of the foothills. No people. Only the birds circling, crying to each other, curious about the car. Only the scurrying animals of the underbrush below.

A little of the tension drained from him as he climbed. Perhaps in these very hills men like him had walked, not many generations ago. Perhaps they would walk there again, amid the disorder of tree and canyon and tumbled rock. Amid the wildness, the beauty that was neither that of the gardens nor that of the old race's cities, but older, more enduring than either.

Below him were other streams, but these were swift-flowing, violent, sparkling like prismed sunlight as they cascaded over the rocks. Their wildness called to him, soothed him as the starship soothed him, as the gardens and the neat domed houses never could.

He knew why his kind had fled to the hills, for whatever little time they had. He knew too that he would come again.

Searching. Looking for his own kind.

That was what he was doing. That was what he had always intended to do, ever since he had heard of the others like himself, the men who had come here before him. He realized his motive suddenly, and realized too the futility of it. But futile or not, he would come again.

For he was of the old race. He shared their hungering.

*   *   *   *   *

Walden was reading in his study when the council members arrived. They came without advance warning and filed in ceremoniously, responding rather coolly to his greeting.

"We're here about the boy," Abbot began abruptly. "He's at the museum now, isn't he?"

Walden nodded. "He's been spending most of his time there lately."

"Do you think it's wise, letting him wander around alone?"

Trouble. Always trouble. Just because there was one young boy, Eric, asking only to be let alone. And the old council members wouldn't rest until they had managed to find an excuse to put him in an institution somewhere, where his actions could be watched, where there wouldn't be any more uncertainty.

"Eric's all right."

"Is he? Prior tells me he leaves the museum every day. He doesn't come here. He doesn't visit his family."

The thin man, Drew, broke in. "He goes to the hills. Just like the others did. Did you know that, Walden?"

Walden's mouth tightened. It wouldn't do to let them read his hostility to their prying. It would be even worse to let them know that they worried him.

"Besides," Drew added, "he's old enough to be thinking about women now. There's always a chance he'll—"

"Are you crazy?" Walden shouted the words aloud. "Eric's not an animal."

"Isn't he?" Abbot answered quietly. "Weren't all the old race just animals?"

Walden turned away from them, closing his mind to their thoughts. He mustn't show anger. If he did, they'd probably decide he was too emotional, not to be trusted. They'd take Eric away, to some institution. Cage him....

"What do you want to do with the boy?" Walden forced his thoughts to come quietly. "Do you want to put him in a zoo with the other animals?"

The sarcasm hurt them. They wanted to be fair. Abbot especially prided himself on his fairness.

"Of course not."

They hesitated. They weren't going to do anything. Not this time. They stood around and made a little polite conversation, about other things, and then Abbot turned toward the door.

"We just wanted to be sure you knew what was going on." Abbot paused. "You'll keep an eye on the boy, won't you?"

"Am I his keeper?" Walden asked softly.

They didn't answer him. Their thoughts were confused and a bit irritated as they went out to the aircar that had brought them. But he knew they'd be back. And they would keep track of Eric. Prior, the caretaker, would help them. Prior was old too, and worried....

Walden walked back into his study, slowly. His legs were trembling. He hadn't realized how upset he had been. He smiled at the intensity of his emotions, realizing something he'd always kept hidden, even from himself.

He was as fond of Eric as if the boy had been his own son.

*   *   *   *   *

Eric pushed the books away, impatiently. He didn't feel like studying. The equations were meaningless. He was tired of books, and history, and all the facts about the old race.

He wanted to be outdoors, exploring, walking along the hillsides, looking for his own kind.

But he had already explored the hills. He had flown for miles, and walked for miles, and searched dozens of caves in dozens of gorges. He had found no one. He was sure that if there had been anyone he would have discovered some sign.

He opened the book again, but he couldn't concentrate on it.

Beyond those hills, across another valley, there were even higher mountains. He had often looked across at them, wondering what they held. They were probably as desolate as the ones he'd searched. Still, he would rather be out in them, looking, than sitting here, fretting, almost hating the old race because it had somehow bequeathed him a heritage of loneliness.

He got up abruptly and went outside to the aircar.

It was a long way to the second range of mountains. He flew there directly, skimming over the nearer hills, the ones he had spent weeks exploring. He dropped low over the intervening valley, passing over the houses and towns, looking down at the gardens. The new race filled all the valleys.

He came into the foothills and swung the car upward, climbing over the steep mountainsides. Within a mile from the valley's edge he was in wild country. He'd thought the other hills were wild, but here the terrain was jagged and rock-strewn, with boulders flung about as if by some giant hand. There were a hundred narrow canyons, opening into each other, steep-sloped, overgrown with brambles and almost impenetrable, a maze with the hills rising around them and cutting off all view of the surrounding country.

Eric dropped down into one of the larger canyons. Immediately he realized how easy it would be to get lost in those hills. There were no landmarks that were not like a hundred jutting others. Without the aircar he would be lost in a few minutes. He wondered suddenly if anyone, old race or new, had ever been here before him.

He set the aircar down on the valley floor and got out and walked away from it, upstream, following the little creek that tumbled past him over the rocks. By the time he had gone a hundred paces the car was out of sight.

It was quiet. Far away birds called to each other, and insects buzzed around him, but other than these sounds there was nothing but his own footsteps and the creek rapids. He relaxed, walking more slowly, looking about him idly, no longer searching for anything.

He rounded another bend, climbed up over a rock that blocked his path and dropped down on the other side of it. Then he froze, staring.

Not ten feet ahead of him lay the ashes of a campfire, still smoldering, still sending a thin wisp of smoke up into the air.

He saw no one. Nothing moved. No tracks showed in the rocky ground. Except for the fire, the gorge looked as uninhabited as any of the others.

Slowly Eric walked toward the campfire and knelt down and held his hand over the embers. Heat rose about him. The fire hadn't been out for very long.

He turned quickly, glancing about him, but there was no sudden motion anywhere, no indication that anyone was hiding nearby. Perhaps there was nobody near. Perhaps whoever had built the fire had left it some time before, and was miles away by now....

He didn't think so. He had a feeling that eyes were watching him. It was a strange feeling, almost as if he could perceive. Wishful thinking, he told himself. Unreal, untrue....

But *someone* had been here. Someone had built the fire. And it was probably, almost certainly, someone without perception. Someone like himself.

His knees were shaking. His hands trembled, and sweat broke out on the palms. Yet his thoughts seemed calm, icily calm. It was just a nervous reaction, he knew that. A reaction to the sudden knowledge that people *were* here, out in these hills where he had searched for them but never, deep down, expected to find them. They were probably watching him right now, hidden up among the trees somewhere, afraid to move because then he would see them and start out to capture them.

If there were people here, they must think that he was one of the normal ones. That he could perceive. So they would keep quiet, because a person with perception couldn't possibly perceive a person who lacked it. They would remain motionless, hoping to stay hidden, waiting for him to leave so that they could flee deeper into the hills.

They couldn't know that he was one of them.

He felt helpless, suddenly. So near, so near—and yet he couldn't reach them. The people who lived here in the wild mountain gorges could elude him forever.

No motion. No sound. Only the embers, smoking....

"Listen," he called aloud. "Can you hear me?"

The canyon walls caught his voice, sent it echoing back, fainter and fainter. "... can you hear me can you hear me can you...."

No one answered.

"I'm your friend," he called. "I can't perceive. I'm one of you."

Over and over it echoed. "... one of you one of you one of you...."

"Answer me. I've run away from them too. Answer me!"

"Answer me answer me answer me...."

The echoes died away and it was quiet, too quiet. No sound. Even if they heard him, they wouldn't answer.

He couldn't track them. If they had homes that were easy to find they would have left them by now. He was helpless.

The heat from the fire rose about him, and he tasted smoke and coughed. Nothing moved. Finally he stood up, turned away from the fire and walked on past it, up the stream.

No one. No tracks. No sign. Only the feeling that other eyes watched him as he walked along, other ears listened for the sound of his passing.

He turned back, retraced his steps to the fire. The embers had blackened. The wisp of smoke that curled upward was very thin now. Otherwise everything was the same as it had been.

He couldn't give up and fly back to the museum. If he did he might never find them again. But even if he didn't, he might never find them.

"Listen!" He screamed the word, so loudly that they could have heard it miles away. "I'm one of you. I can't perceive. Believe me! You've got to believe me!"

"Believe me believe me believe me...."

Nothing. The tension went out of him suddenly and he began to tremble again, and his throat choked up, wanting to cry. He stumbled away from the embers, back in the direction of the aircar.

"Believe me...." This time the words were little more than a whisper, and there was no echo.

"I believe you," a voice said quietly.

*   *   *   *   *

He swung about, trying to place it, and saw the woman. She stood at the edge of the trees, above the campfire, half hidden in the undergrowth. She looked down at him warily, a rock clenched in her hand. She wasn't an attractive sight.

She looked old, with a leathery skin and gnarled arms and legs. Her grey-white hair was matted, pulled back into a snarled bun behind her head. She wore a shapeless dress of some roughwoven material that hung limply from her shoulders, torn, dirty, ancient. He'd never seen an animal as dirty as she.

"So you can't perceive," the woman cackled. "I believe it, boy. You don't have that look about you."

"I didn't know," Eric said softly. "I never knew until today that there were any others."

She laughed, a high-pitched laugh that broke off into a choking cough. "There aren't many of us, boy. Not many. Me and Nell—but she's an old, old woman. And Lisa, of course...."

She cackled again, nodding. "I always told Lisa to wait," she said firmly. "I told her that there'd be another young one along."

"Who are you?" Eric said.

"Me? Call me Mag. Come on, boy. Come on. What are you waiting for?"

She turned and started off up the hill, walking so fast that she was almost out of sight among the trees before Eric recovered enough to follow her. He stumbled after her, clawing his way up the steep slope, slipping and grabbing the branches with his hands and hauling himself up the rocks.

"You're a slow one." The old woman paused and waited for him to catch up. "Where've you been all your life? You don't act like a mountain boy."

"I'm not," Eric said. "I'm from the valley...."

He stopped talking. He realized, suddenly, the futility of trying to explain his life to her. If she had ever known the towns, it would have been years ago. She was too old, and tattered, and so dirty that her smell wasn't even a good clean animal smell.

"Hurry up, boy!"

He felt unreal, as if this were a dream, as if he would awaken suddenly and be back at the museum. He almost wished that he would. He couldn't believe that he had found another like himself and was now following her, scrambling up a mountain as if he were a goat.

A goat. Smells. The dirty old woman in front of him. He wrinkled his nose in disgust and then was furious with himself, with his reactions, with the sudden knowledge that he had glamorized his kind and had hoped to find them noble and brilliant.

This tattered old woman with her cackling laugh and leathery, toothless face and dirt encrusted clothing couldn't be like him. He couldn't accept it....

Mag led him up the slope and then over some heaped boulders, and suddenly they were on level ground again. They had come out into a tiny canyon, a blind pocket recessed into the mountain, almost completely surrounded by walls that rose sharply upward. Back across the gorge, huddled against the face of the mountain, was a tiny hut.

It was primitive, like those in the prehistoric sections of the old history books. It was made of branches lashed together, with sides that leaned crookedly against each other and a matted roof that looked as if it would slide off at any minute. It was like a twig house that a child might make with sticks and grass.

"Our home," Mag said. Her voice was proud.

He didn't answer. He followed her across toward it, past the mounds of refuse, the fruit rinds and bones and skins that were flung carelessly beside the trail. He smelled the scent of decay and rottenness and turned his head away, feeling sick.

"Lisa! Lisa!" Mag shouted, the words echoing and re-echoing.

A figure moved just inside the hut doorway. "She's not here," a voice called. "She's out hunting."

"Well, come on out, Nell, and see what I've found."

The figure moved slowly out from the gloom of the hut, bending to get through the low door, half straightening up outside, and Eric saw that it was an old, old woman. She couldn't straighten very far. She was too old, bent and twisted and brittle, feebler looking than anyone Eric had ever seen before. She hobbled toward him slowly, teetering from side to side as she walked, her hands held out in front of her, her eyes on the ground.

"What is it, Mag?" Her voice was as twisted as her body.

"A boy. Valley boy. Just the age for our Lisa, too."

Eric felt his face redden and he opened his mouth to protest, to say something, anything, but Mag went right on talking, ignoring him.

"The boy came in an aircar. I thought he was one of the normals—but he's not. Hasn't their ways. Good looking boy, too."

"Is he?" Nell had reached them. She stopped and looked up, right into Eric's face, and for the first time he realized that she was blind. Her eyes were milky white, without pupils, without irises. Against the brown leather of her skin they looked moist and dead.

"Speak, boy," she croaked. "Let me hear your voice."

"Hello," Eric said, feeling utterly foolish and utterly confused. "I'm Eric."

"Eric...." Nell reached out, touched his arm with her hand, ran her fingers up over his shoulders, over his chest.

"It's been a long time since I've heard a man's voice," she said. "Not since Mag here was a little girl."

"Have you been—here—all that time?" Eric asked, looking around him at the hut, and the meat hanging to dry, covered with flies, and the leather water bags, and the mounds of refuse, the huge, heaped mounds that he couldn't stop smelling.

"Yes," Nell said. "I've been here longer than I want to remember, boy. We came here from the other mountains when Mag was only a baby."

* * * * *

They walked toward the hut, and as they neared it he smelled a new smell, that of stale smoke and stale sweat overlying the general odor of decay.

"Let's talk out here," he said, not wanting to go inside.

They sat down on the hard earth and the two women turned their faces toward him, Mag watching him intently, Nell listening, her head cocked to one side like an old crippled bird's.

"I always thought I was the only one like me," Eric said. "The people don't know of any others. They don't know you exist. They wouldn't believe it."

"That's the way we want it," Mag said. "That's the only way it can be."

Nell nodded. "I was a girl in the other hills," she said, nodding toward the west, toward the museum. "There were several of us then. There had been families of us in my father's time, and in his father's time, and maybe before that even. But when I was a girl there was only my father and my mother and another wife of my father's, and a lot of children...."

She paused, still looking toward the west, facing a horizon she could no longer see. "The normal ones came. We'd hidden from them before. But this time we had no chance to hide. I was hunting, with the boy who was my father's nephew.

"They surrounded the hut. They didn't make any sound. They don't have to. I was in the forest when I heard my mother scream."

"Did they kill her?" Eric cried out. "They wouldn't do that."

"No, they didn't kill any of them. They dragged them off to the aircars, all of them. My father, my mother and the other woman, the children. We watched from the trees and saw them dragged off, tied with ropes, like wild animals. The cars flew away. Our people never came back."

She stopped, sunken in revery. Mag took up the story. Her voice was matter-of-fact, completely casual about those long ago events.

"A bear killed my father. That was after we came back here. Nell was sick. I did the hunting. We almost starved, for a while, but there's lots of game in the hills. It's a good life here. But I've been sorry for Lisa. She's a woman now. She needs a man. I'm glad you came. I would have hated to send her out looking for a normal one."

"But—" Eric stopped, his head whirling. He didn't know what to say. Anything at all would sound wrong, cruel.

"It's dangerous," Mag went on, "taking up with the normals. They think it's wrong. They think we're animals. One of us has to pick a man who's stupid—a farmer, maybe—and even then it's like being a pet. A beast."

It took a moment for Eric to realize what she was saying, and when he did realize, the thought horrified him.

"Lisa's father was stupid," Mag said. "He took me in when I came down from the hills. He didn't send for the others. Not then. He kept me and fed me and treated me kindly, and I thought I was safe. I thought our kind and theirs could live together."

She laughed. Deep, bitter lines creased her mouth. "A week later the aircar came. They sneaked up to the garden where I was. He was with them. He was leading them."

She laughed again. "Their kindness means nothing. Their love means nothing. To them, we're animals."

The old woman, Nell, rocked back and forth, her face still in revery. Flies crawled over her bare arms, unheeded.

"I got away," Mag said. "I saw them coming. They can't run fast, and I knew the hiding places. I never went back to the valleys. Nell would have starved without me. And there was Lisa to care for, later...."

The flies settled on Eric's hands and he brushed them away, shivering.

Mag smiled. The bitterness left her face. "I'm glad I don't have to send Lisa down to the valley."

She got up before he could answer, before he could even think of anything to say or do. Crossing over to the pole where the dried meat hung, she pulled a piece of it loose and brought it back to where they sat. Some she gave to the old woman and some she kept for herself and the rest, most of it, she tossed to Eric.

"You must be hungry, boy."

It was filthy. Dirt clung to it—dust and pollen and grime—and the flies had flown off in clouds when she lifted it down.

The old woman raised her piece and put the edge of it in her mouth and started to chew, slowly, eating her way up the strip. Mag tore hers with her teeth, rending it and swallowing it quickly, watching Eric all the time.

"Eat."

It was unreal. He couldn't be here. These women couldn't exist.

He lifted the meat, feeling his stomach knot with disgust, wanting to fling it from him and run, blindly, down the hill to the aircar. But he didn't. He had searched too long to flee now. Shuddering, he closed his mind to the flies and the smell and the filth and bit into the meat and chewed it and swallowed it. And all the time, Mag watched him.

The sun passed overhead and began to dip toward the west. The shadows, which had shortened as they sat in front of the hut, lengthened again, until they themselves were half in the shadow of the trees lining the gorge. Still Lisa did not come. It was very quiet. The only sounds that broke the silence were their own voices and the buzzing of the flies.

They talked, but communication was difficult between them. Eric tried to accept their ideas, their way of life, but he couldn't. The things they said were strange to him. Their whole pattern of life was strange to him. He could understand it at all only because he had studied the primitive peoples of the old race. But he couldn't imagine himself as one of them. He couldn't think of himself as having grown up among them, in the hills, living only to hunt and gather berries and store food for the wintertime. He couldn't think of himself hiding, creeping through the gorges like a hunted animal, flattening himself in the underbrush whenever an aircar passed by.

He sat and listened to them talk, and his amazement grew. Their beliefs were so different. He listened to their superstitious accounts of the old race, and the way it had been "in the beginning."

He listened to their legends of the old gods who flew through the air and were a mighty people, but who were destroyed by a new race of devils. He listened as they told him of their own ancestors, children of the gods, who had fled to the hills to await the gods' return. They had no conception at all of the thousands of years that had elapsed between the old race's passing and their own forefathers' flight into the hills. And when he tried to explain, they shook their heads and wouldn't believe him.

He didn't hear Lisa come. One minute the far end of the clearing was empty and still and the next minute the girl was walking across it toward them, a bow in one hand and a pair of rabbits dangling from the other.

She saw him and stopped, the rabbits dropping from her hand.

"Here's your young man, Lisa," Mag said. "Valley boy. His name's Eric."

He stared back at her, more in curiosity than in surprise. She wasn't nearly as unattractive as he had thought she would be. She wouldn't be bad looking at all, he thought, if she were clean. She was fairly tall and lean, too skinny really, with thin muscular arms instead of the softly rounded arms the valley girls had. She was too brown, but her skin hadn't turned leathery yet, and there was still a little life in the lank brown hair that fell matted about her shoulders.

"Hello, Lisa," he said.

"Hello." Her eyes never left him. She stared at him, her lips trembling, her whole body tensed. She looked as if she were going to turn and run at any moment, as if only his quietness kept her from fleeing.

With a sudden shock Eric realized that she too was afraid—afraid of him. His own hesitation fell away and he smiled at her.

Mag got up and went over to the girl and put her arm around Lisa's shoulders. "Don't be afraid of him, child," Mag said. "He's a nice boy. Not like one of *them*."

Lisa trembled.

Eric watched her, pitying her. She was as helpless as he before the calm assumption of the older women. More helpless, because she had probably never thought of defying them, of escaping the pattern of their lives.

"Don't worry, Lisa," he said. "I won't hurt you."

Slowly she walked toward him, poised, waiting for a hostile move. She came within a few feet of him and then sank to her haunches, still watching him, still poised.

She was as savage as the others. A graceful, dirty savage.

"You're really one of us?" she said. "You can't perceive?"

"No," he said. "I can't perceive."

"He's not like them," Mag said flatly. "If you'd ever been among them, you'd know their ways."

"I've never seen a man before, up close," Lisa said.

Her eyes pleaded with him, and suddenly he knew why he pitied her. It was because she felt helpless before him, and begged him not to harm her, and thought of him as something above her, more powerful than she, and dangerous. He looked across at her and felt protective, and it was a new feeling to him, absolutely new. Because always before, around the normals, even around his own parents and Walden, he had been the helpless one.

He liked this new feeling, and wished it could last. But it couldn't. He couldn't do as the old women expected him to, leave the valley and his parents, leave the books and the museum and the ship, just to hide in the hills like a beast with them.

He had come to find his people, but these three were not they.

"You two go on off and talk," Mag said. "We're old. We don't matter now. You've got things to settle between you."

She cackled again and got up and went into the hut and old Nell got up also and followed her.

The girl shivered. She drew back a little, away from him. Her eyes never left his face.

"Don't be afraid, Lisa," he said gently. "I won't hurt you. I won't even touch you. But I would like to talk to you."

"All right," she said.

They got up and walked to the end of the gorge, the girl keeping always a few feet from him. At the boulders she stopped and faced him, her back against a rock, her thin body still trembling.

"Lisa," he said. "I want to be your friend."

Her eyes widened. "How can you?" she said. "Men are friends. Women are friends. But you're a man and I'm a woman and it's different."

He shook his head helplessly, trying to think of a way to explain things to her. He couldn't say that he found her dirty and unattractive and almost another species. He couldn't say that he'd searched the hills, often thinking of the relationship between man and woman, but that she wasn't the woman, that she never could be the woman for him. He couldn't tell her that he pitied her in perhaps the same way that the normals pitied him.

Still, he wanted to talk to her. He wanted to be her friend. Because he was sure now that he could search the mountains forever, and perhaps find other people, even if those he found were like her, and Mag and Nell.

"Listen, Lisa," he said. "I can't live up here. I live in the valley. I came in an aircar, and it's down in the canyon below here. I have to go back—soon. Before it gets completely dark."

"Why?"

"If I don't the normals will come looking for me. They'll find the aircar and then they'll find us. And you and your family will be taken away. Don't you understand?"

"You're going?" Lisa said.

"In a little while. I must."

She looked at him, strangely. She looked at his clothes, at his face, at his body. Then she looked at her own hands and touched her own coarse dress, and she nodded.

"You won't come back," she said. "You don't like me. I'm not what you were searching for."

He couldn't answer. Her words hurt him. The very fact that she could recognize their difference from each other hurt him. He pitied her still more.

"I'll come back," he said, "Of course I will. As often as I can. You're the only other people I've ever known who didn't perceive."

She looked up into his face again. Her eyes were very large. They were the only beautiful thing about her.

"Even if you do come back, you won't want me."

There wasn't any answer at all.

*   *   *   *   *

It was dusk when Eric got back to the museum. He landed the aircar and climbed out and walked across to the building, still feeling unreal, still not believing that the events of this day had actually happened.

He nodded to Prior and the old caretaker nodded back and then stood staring at him, troubled and curious. Eric didn't notice the other's expression, nor the fact that Prior followed him to the top of the spiral ramp and remained there for a while, watching.

Eric stood at the bottom of the well where he had so often stood before, staring across at the ship, then looking up, up, up its sleek length to where its nose pointed yearningly toward the night sky. But tonight he found no comfort in the sight, no sense of kinship with its builders. Tonight the ship was a dead and empty thing.

"*You won't want me*—" Her voice, her eyes, came between him and the stars.

He had thought of finding his people and sharing with them their common heritage from the past, the knowledge of the old race and its thoughts and its science and its philosophy. He had thought of sharing with them the old desire for the stars, the old hunger, the old loneliness that the new race could never understand. He had been wrong.

His people.... He pushed the thought away.

He looked up at the stars that were merely pin-pricks of light at the top of the well and wondered if anyone, old race or new or something different from either, lived among them now. And he felt small, and even the ship was small, and his own problems and his own search were unimportant. He sat down and leaned back against the smooth wall and closed his eyes, blotting out the ship and the stars, and finally, even Lisa's face before him.

The old caretaker found him sleeping there, and sighed, and went away again, still frowning. Eric slept on, unheeding. When he awoke it was late morning and the stars were gone and clouds drifted across the mouth of the well.

There was no answer here. The starship would never fly.

And Eric went back to the mountains.

*   *   *   *   *

It was two weeks later that the councilmen stood facing Walden across the great museum table. They had come together, Abbot and Drew and the others, and they faced him together, frowning. Their thoughts were hidden. Walden could catch only glimpses of what lay beneath their worry.

"Every day." Abbot's eyes were hard, unyielding. "Why, Walden? Why does he go there every day?"

"Does it matter?"

"Perhaps. Perhaps not. We can't tell—yet."

The ring of faces, of buried perceptions, of fear, anxiety, and a worry that could no longer be shrugged off. And Eric away, as he was every day now, somewhere in the distant hills.

"The boy's all right." Walden checked his own rush of worry.

"Is he?"

The worry in the open now, the fear uncontained, and no more vacillation. Their thoughts hidden from Walden, their plans hidden, and nothing he could do, no way to warn Eric, yet.

Abbot smiled, humorlessly. "The boy had better be all right...."

*   *   *   *   *

Eric landed in the canyon and made sure that the aircar was hidden under a ledge, with branches drawn about it so that no one could spot it from above. Then he turned and started for the slope, and as he reached it Lisa ran down to meet him.

"You're late," she called.

"Am I? Have you really been waiting for me?"

"Of course." She came over to meet him, laughing, openly glad that he had come.

He smiled back at her and walked along beside her, having to take long strides to match her skipping ones, and he too was glad that he'd come. Lately he felt like this every day. It was a feeling he couldn't analyze. Nothing had changed. The girl was still too thin and too brown and too dirty, although now she had begun to wash her dress and her body in the mountain stream and to comb the snarls from her hair. But it didn't make her attractive to him. It only made her less unattractive.

"Will you always have to go away every night?" she asked guilelessly.

"I suppose so."

He looked down at her and smiled, wondering why he came. There was still an air of unreality about the whole situation. He felt numb. He had felt that way ever since the first day, and the feeling had grown, until now he moved and spoke and smiled and ate and it was as if he were someone else and the person he had been was gone completely. He liked coming here. But there was no triumph in being with these people, no sense of having found his own kind, no purpose, nothing but a vague contentment and an unwillingness to search any farther.

"You're very quiet," Lisa said.

"I know. I was thinking."

She reached out and touched his arm, her fingers strong and muscular. He smiled at her but made no move toward her, and after a moment she sighed and took her hand away.

"Why are you so different, Eric?"

"Perhaps because I was raised by the others, the normal ones. Perhaps just because I've read so many books about the old race...."

They came up to the boulders that blocked the entrance of the little gorge where the hut was. Lisa started toward them, then stopped abruptly.

"Let's go on up the hill. I want to talk to you, without them."

"All right."

He followed her without speaking, concentrating all his effort on scrambling over the rougher spots in the trail. She didn't say anything more until they had come out on a high ledge that overlooked the whole canyon and she had sat down and motioned for him to sit down too.

"Whew," he panted. "You're a mountain goat, Lisa."

She didn't smile. "I've liked your coming to see us," she said. "I like to listen to you talk. I like the tales you tell of the old ones. But Mag and Nell are upset."

He knew what was coming. His eyes met hers, and then he looked away and reddened and felt sorry for her and what he would have to tell her. This was a subject they had managed to avoid ever since that first day, although the older women brought it up whenever he saw them.

"Mag says I must have a man," Lisa said. Her voice was tight. He couldn't tell if she was crying because he couldn't bear to look at her. He could only stare out over the canyon and listen and wait.

"She says if it isn't you I'll have to find someone else, later on, but she says it ought to be you. Because *they're* dangerous, and besides, if it's you our children will be sure to be like us."

"What?" He swung around, startled. "Do you mean that if one parent were normal the child might be too?"

"Yes," she said. "It might. They say that's happened. Sometimes. No one knows why we're born. No one knows why some are one way and some another."

"Lisa...." He stopped.

"I know. You don't want me. I've known that all the time."

"It isn't just that."

He tried to find the words to express what he felt, but anything he might say would be cold and cruel and not quite true. He felt the contentment drain out of him, and he felt annoyed, because he didn't want to have to think about her problem, or about anything.

"Why do they want you to have a child?" he said roughly. "Why do they want our kind to go on, living here like animals, or taken to the valleys and separated from each other and put into institutions until we die? Why don't they admit that we've lost, that the normals own the Earth? Why don't they stop breeding and let us die?"

"Your parents were normal, Eric. If all of us died, others would be born, someday."

He nodded and then he closed his eyes and fought against the despair that rose suddenly within him and blotted out the last of the contentment and the unreality. He fought against it and lost. And suddenly Lisa was very real, more real even than the books had ever been. And the dirty old women were suddenly people—individuals, not savages. He tried to pity them, to retreat into his pity and his loneliness, but he couldn't even do that.

The people he had looked for were imaginary. He would never find them, because Mag and Nell and Lisa

were his people. They were like him, and the only
difference between him and them was one of luck. They
were dirty and ignorant. They had been born in the
mountains and hunted like beasts. He was more
fortunate; he had been born in the valley.

He was a snob. He had looked down on them, when all
the time he was one of them. If he had been born among
them, he would have been as they were. And, if Lisa had
lived in another age, she too would have sought the stars.

Eric sat very still and fought until a little of the
turmoil quieted inside of him. Then he opened his eyes
again and stared across the canyon, at the rock slides and
the trees growing out from the slopes at twisting,
precarious angles, and he saw everything in a new light.
He saw the old race as it had been far earlier than the
age of space-travel, and he knew that it had conquered
many environments on Earth before it had gained a
chance to try for those of space. He felt humble, suddenly,
and proud at the same time.

Lisa sat beside him, not speaking, drawing away from
him and letting him be by himself, as if she knew the
conflicts within him and knew enough not to interrupt.
He was grateful both for her presence there beside him
and for her silence.

Much later, when afternoon shadows had crept well
out from the rocks, she turned to him. "Will you take me
to the valley someday, Eric?"

"Maybe. But no one must know about you. You know
what would happen if any of them found out you even
existed."

"Yes," she said. "We'd have to be careful, all right. But
you could take me for a ride in the aircar sometime and
show me things."

Before, he would have shrugged off her words and
forgotten them. Now he couldn't. Decision crystalized
quickly in his mind.

"Come on, Lisa," he said, getting to his feet and reaching down to help her up also. "I'll take you to the valley right now."

She looked up at him, unable to speak, her eyes shining, and then she was running ahead of him, down the slope toward the aircar.

*   *   *   *   *

The car climbed swiftly away from the valley floor, up between the canyon walls and above them, over the crest of the hills. He circled it for a moment, banking it over on its side so that she could look down at the gorge and the rocks and the cascading stream.

"How do you like it, Lisa?"

"I don't know." She smiled, rather weakly, her body braced against the seat. "It feels so strange."

He smiled back and straightened the car, turning away from the mountains until the great, gardened valley stretched out before them, all the way to the foot of the western hills.

"I'll show you the museum," he said. "I only wish I could take you inside."

She moved away from him, nearer to the window, and looked down at the scattered houses that lay below them, at the people moving in the gardens, at the children.

"I never dreamed it was like this," she said. "I never could picture it before."

There was a longing in her face he'd never noticed before. He stared at her, and she was different suddenly, and her thin muscular body was different too.

Pioneer—that was the word he wanted.

The girls of the new race could never be pioneers.

"Look, Eric. Over there. Aircars."

The words broke in on his thoughts and he looked away from her, following her gaze incuriously, not much interested. And then his fingers stiffened on the controls and the peacefulness fell away from him as if it had never been.

"Lots of them," she said.

Aircars. Eight or ten of them, more than he had ever seen at one time, spread out in a line and flying eastward, straight toward him.

They mustn't see Lisa. They mustn't get close enough to realize who he was.

He swung away from them, perpendicular to their course, angling so that he would be out of perception range, and then he circled, close to the ground, as they swept by, undeviating, purposeful, toward the mountains.

Toward the mountains.

Fear. Sudden, numbing fear and the realization of his own carelessness.

"What's the matter, Eric?"

He had swung about and now followed them, far behind them and off to one side, much too far away for them to try to perceive him. Perhaps, he thought, perhaps they don't know. But all the time he remembered his own trips to the canyon, taken so openly.

"Oh, Eric, they're not—"

He swung up over the last ridge and looked down, and her words choked off in her throat. Below them lay the canyon, and in it, the long line of aircars, landed now, cutting off the gorge, the light reflecting off them, bronze in the sunset. And the tiny figures of men were even now spreading out from the cars.

"What'll we do, Eric?"

Panic. In her voice and in her eyes and in her fingers that bit into his arm, hurting him, steadying him against his own fear and the twisting realization of his betraying lack of caution.

"Run. What else can we do?"

Down back over the ridge, out of sight of the aircars and into the foothills, and all the while knowing that there was nowhere to run to now.

"No, Eric! We've got to go back. We've got to find Mag and Nell—" Her voice rose in anguish, then broke, and she was crying.

"We can't help them by going back," he said harshly. "Maybe they got away. Maybe they didn't. But the others would catch us for sure if they got near us."

Run. It was all they could do, now. Run to other hills and leave the aircar and hide, and live as Lisa had lived, as others of their kind had lived.

"We've got to think of ourselves, Lisa. It's all we can do, now."

Down through the foothills, toward the open valley, and the future, the long blind race to other mountains, and no choice left, no alternative, and the books lost and the starship left behind, forever....

Lisa cried, and her fingers bit into his arm. Ahead of him, too close to flee or deceive, was another line of aircars, flying in from the valley, their formation breaking as they veered toward him.

"Land, Eric. Land and run!"

"We can't, Lisa. There's not enough time."

Everything was lost now—even the hills.

Unless ... one chance. The only chance, and it was nearly hopeless.

"Get in the back, Lisa," he said. "Climb over the seat and hide in that storage compartment. And stay there."

The two nearest cars had swung about now and paralleled his course, flanking him, drifting in nearer and nearer.

"Why?" Lisa clung to him. "What are you going to do?"

"They don't know you're with me. They probably don't even know I went back to the canyon. They think I'll land at the museum, not suspecting anything's wrong. So I'll do just what they expect me to. Go back, and pretend I don't know a thing."

"You're mad."

"It's our only chance, Lisa. If only they don't lock me up tonight...."

She clung to him for still another minute and then she climbed over the seat and he heard the luggage compartment panel slide open and, a moment later, shut.

The nearest aircar drifted still closer to him, escorting him west-ward, toward the museum. Behind him, other cars closed in.

*   *   *   *   *

Walden and Prior were waiting for him at the entrance of the main building, just as they had waited so often before. He greeted them casually, trying to act exactly as he usually did, but their greetings to him were far from casual. They stared at him oddly, Prior even drawing back a little as he approached. Walden looked at him for a long moment, very seriously, as if trying to tell him something, but what it was Eric didn't know. Both men were worried, their anxiety showing in their manner, and Eric wondered if he himself showed the fear that gripped him.

They must know what had happened. By now probably every normal person within a hundred miles of the museum must know.

At the entrance he glanced back idly and saw that one of the aircars that had followed him had landed and that the others were angling off again, leaving. It was too dark to see how many men got out of the car, but Walden and Prior were facing in that direction, communicating, and Eric knew that they knew. Everything.

It was like a trap around him, with each of their minds a strand of the net, and he was unable to see which strands were about to entangle him, unable to see if there were any holes through which he might escape. All he could do was pretend that he didn't even know the net existed, and wait.

Half a dozen men came up to Prior and Walden. One of them was Abbot. His face was very stern, and when he glanced over at where Eric stood in the building entrance his face grew even sterner.

Eric watched them for a moment; then he went inside, the way he usually did when there were lots of people around. He wished he knew what they were saying. He wished he knew what was going to happen.

He went on into the library and pulled out a book at random and sat down and started turning the pages. He couldn't read. He kept waiting for them to come in, for one of them to lay a hand on his shoulder and tell him to come along, that they knew he had found other people like himself and that he was a danger to their race and that they were going to lock him up somewhere.

What would happen to Lisa? They'd find her, of course. She could never escape alone, on foot, to the hills.

What had happened to Mag and Nell?

No one came. He knew that their perceptions lay all around him, but he could sense no emotions, no thoughts but his own.

He sat and waited, his eyes focused on the book but not seeing it. It seemed hours before anyone came. Then Prior and Abbot and Walden were in the archway, looking across at him. Prior's face was still worried, Abbot's stern, Walden's reassuring....

Eric forced himself to smile at them and then turn another page and pretend to go on reading. After a moment he heard their footsteps retreating, and when he looked up again they were gone.

He sat a while longer and then he got up and walked down the ramp and stood for a few minutes looking at the ship, because that too would be expected of him. He felt nothing. The ship was a world away now, mocking him, for his future no longer lay in the past, with the old race, but out in the hills. If he had a future at all....

He went up the ramp again, toward his own room. No one else was in sight. They had all gone to bed, perhaps. They wouldn't expect him to try to run away now.

He began to walk, as aimlessly as he could, in the direction of the aircar. He saw no one. Perhaps it wasn't even guarded. He circled around it, still seeing no one; then, feeling more secure suddenly, he went directly toward it and reached up to open the panel and climb in.

"Is that you, Eric?"

Walden's voice. Quiet as always. And it came from inside the car.

*   *   *   *   *

Eric stood frozen, looking up at the ship, trying to see Walden's face and unable to find it in the darkness. He didn't answer—couldn't answer. He listened, and heard nothing except Walden, there above him, moving on the seat.

Where was Lisa?

"I thought you'd come back here," Walden said. He climbed down out of the aircar and stood facing Eric, his body a dim shadow.

"Why are you here?" Eric whispered.

"I wanted to see you. Without the others knowing it. I was sure you'd come here tonight."

Walden. Always Walden. First his teacher and then his friend, and now the one man who stood between him and freedom. For a second Eric felt his muscles tense and he stiffened, ready to leap upon the older man and knock him down and take the ship and run. Then he relaxed. It was a senseless impulse, primitive and useless.

"The others don't know you have any idea what's happened, Eric. But I could tell. It was written all over you."

"What did they find, Walden?"

The old man sighed, and when he spoke his voice was very tired. "They found two women. They tried to capture them, but the women ran out on a ledge. The older one slipped and fell and the other tried to catch her and she fell too. They were dead when the men reached them."

Eric listened, and slowly his tension relaxed, replaced by a dull ache of mourning. But he knew that he was glad to hear that they were dead and not captured, not dragged away from the hills to be bathed and well fed and imprisoned forever under the eyes of the new race.

"The old one was blind," Walden said. "It may have been her blindness that caused her to fall."

"It wasn't."

"No, Eric, it probably wasn't."

They were silent for a moment, and there was no sound at all except for their own breathing. Eric wondered if Lisa still hid in the aircar, if she was listening to them, afraid and hopeless and crying over the death of her people.

"Why did you come out here, Walden?"

"To see you. I came today, when I realized how suspicious the council had grown. I was going to warn you, to tell you to keep away from the hills, that they wanted an excuse to lock you up. I was too late."

"I was careless, Walden." He felt guilt twist inside of him.

"No. You didn't know the danger. I should have warned you sooner. But I never dreamed you would find anyone in the hills, Eric. I never dreamed there were any more without perception, this generation."

Eric moved nearer the car and leaned against it, the cold plastic next to his body cooling him a little, steadying him against the feverish trembling that shook his legs and sent sweat down over him and made him too weak, suddenly, to want to struggle further.

"Let me go, Walden. Let me take the car and go."

Walden didn't move. He stood quietly, a tall thin shape in the darkness.

"There are other people the searchers didn't find, aren't there? And you're going to them."

Eric didn't answer. He looked past Walden, at the car, wishing he could somehow call to Lisa, wishing they could perceive so that he could reassure her and promise her that somehow he'd still take her to freedom. But it would be an empty promise....

"I've warned you too late. You've found your people, but it won't do you any good. They'll hunt you through the hills, and I won't be able to help you any more."

Eric looked back at him, hearing the sadness in his voice. It was real sadness, real emotion. He thought of the years he had spent with Walden, learning, absorbing the old race knowledge, and he remembered that all through those years Walden had never once made him feel uncomfortable because of the difference between them.

He looked at the old man for a long time, wishing that it was day so he could read the other's expression, wondering how he had managed to take this man for granted for so long.

"Why?" he whispered. "Why are you helping me? Why aren't you like the others?"

"I never had a son, Eric. Perhaps that's the reason."

Eric thought of Myron and shook his head. "No, it isn't that. My father doesn't feel the way you do. He can't forget that I'm not normal. With him, I'm always aware of the difference."

"And you're not with me?"

"No," Eric said. "I'm not. Why?" And he wondered why he had never asked that question before.

"The final question," Walden said softly. "I wondered how long it would be before you asked it. I wondered if you'd ever ask it.

"Haven't you ever thought about why I never married, Eric? Haven't you ever asked yourself why I alone learned to read, and collected books, and studied the old race?"

"No," Eric admitted. "I just accepted you."

"Even though I can perceive and you can't." Walden paused and Eric waited, not knowing what was coming and yet sure that nothing could surprise him now.

"My father was normal," Walden said slowly. "But I never saw him. My mother was like you. So was my brother. We lived in the hills and I was the only one who could perceive. I learned what it was to be different."

Eric stared. He couldn't stop staring. And yet he should have realized, long ago, that Walden was different too, in his own way.

Walden smiled back, his face, shadowed in moonlight, as quiet and as understanding as ever. For a moment neither spoke, and there was only the faraway sound of crickets chirping and the rustling of the wind in the gardens.

And then, from within the aircar, there was a different rustling, that of a person moving.

"Lisa!"

Eric pushed the compartment panel back. The soft light came on automatically, framing her where she curled against the far wall.

"You heard us?"

She nodded. Tears had dried on her cheeks. Her eyes were huge in her thin face.

"We'd better go, Lisa."

He reached in to help her out.

They didn't see the aircar dropping in for a landing until it was almost upon them, until its lights arced down over the museum walls.

"Hide, Eric. In here—" Lisa pulled him forward.

Behind them, Walden's voice, suddenly tired in the darkness. "It's too late. They know I'm here. And they're wondering why."

The three of them stood frozen, watching each other, while the dark shape of the car settled to the ground some thirty yards away.

"It's Abbot," Walden said. He paused, intent for a moment, and added, "He doesn't know about you. Get out of sight somewhere, both of you, away from here—"

"Come on, Lisa—" Eric swung away from the car, toward the shelter of the building and whatever hiding place there might be. "Hurry!"

They ran, and the museum rose in front of them, and the door was open. They were through it and into the dim corridor, and there was no one around; Walden's figure was lost in the night outside. Beyond the libraries the great ramp spiraled downward.

"This way, Lisa!"

They came out into the bottom of the well and there in front of them the starship rested. Still reaching upward. Still waiting, as it had waited for so many uncounted years.

Their ship—if only it could be their ship....

"Oh, Eric!"

Side by side they stood staring at it, and Eric wished that they could get into it and go, right now, while they were still free and there was no one to stop them. But they couldn't. There was no food in the ship, no plant tanks, none of the many provisions the books listed.

Besides, if they took off now they would destroy the museum and all the people in it, and probably kill themselves as well.

"Eric! We know you're down there!" It wasn't Walden's voice.

Lisa moved closer. Eric put his arm around her and held her while footsteps hurried toward them down the ramp. The council. Abbot and Drew and the others. Prior, shaking his head. Walden.

"Let us go," Eric cried. "Why won't you let us go?"

Walden turned to the others. His eyes pleaded with them. His lips moved and his hands were expressive, gesturing. But the others stood without moving, without expression.

Then Abbot pushed Walden aside and started forward, his face hard and determined and unchangeable.

"You won't let us go," Eric said.

"No. You're fools, both of you."

There was one answer, only one answer, and with it, a hot violence in his blood as the old race pattern came into focus, as the fear and the futility fell away.

It was only a few steps to the ship. Eric caught Lisa's arm and pulled her after him and ran toward it, reaching up to the door. In one motion he flung it open and lifted her through it, then he swung about to face the others.

"Let us go!" he shouted. "Promise to let us go, or we'll take off anyway and if we die at least you'll die too!"

Abbot stopped. He looked back at Walden, his face scornful. "You see?" he said aloud. "They're mad. And you let this happen."

He turned away, dismissing Walden, and came toward the ship. The others followed him.

Eric waited. He stood with his back to the door, waiting, as Abbot strode toward him, ahead of the other councilmen, alone and unprotected.

"You're the fool!" Eric said. He laughed as he leaped forward.

Abbot's eyes went wide suddenly; he tried to dodge, gave a little grunt, and went limp in Eric's grasp.

Eric laughed again, swung Abbot into the ship and leaped in himself. The old race and its violence had never been nearer.

He slammed the door shut, bolted it, and turned back to where the councilman was struggling to his feet.

"Now will you let us go?" Eric said softly. "Or must we take off now, with you—for the stars?"

For a long moment Abbot looked at him, and then his lips trembled and his whole body went slack in defeat.

"The ship is yours," he whispered. "Just let me go."

Outside the ship, Walden chuckled wryly.

*　　*　　*　　*　　*

The Vacuum Suit was strange against Eric's body, as strange as the straps that bound him to the couch. He looked over at Lisa and she too was unrecognizable, a great bloated slug tied down beside him. Only her face, frightened behind the helmet, looked human.

He reached for the controls, then paused, glancing down through the view screens at the ground, at the people two hundred feet below, tiny ants scurrying away from the ship, running to shelter but still looking up at him. He couldn't see his parents or Walden.

His fingers closed about the control lever but still he stared down. Everything that had been familiar all his life stood out sharply now, because he was leaving and it would never be there again for him. And he had to remember what it was like....

Then he looked up. The sky was blue and cloudless above him, and there were no stars at all. But he knew that beyond the sky the stars were shining.

And perhaps, somewhere amid the stars, the old race waited.

He turned to Lisa. "This may be goodbye, darling."

"It may be. But it doesn't matter, really."

They had each other. It was enough. Even though they could never be as close to each other as the new race was close. They were separate, with a gulf always between their inmost thoughts, but they could bridge that gulf, sometimes.

He turned back to the controls and his fingers tightened. The last line of the poem shouted in his mind, and he laughed, for he knew finally what the poet had meant, what the old race had lived for. *We have cast off the planets like outgrown toys, and now we want the stars....*

He pulled the lever back and the ship sprang free. A terrible weight pressed against him, crushing him, stifling him. But still he laughed, because he was one of the old race, and he was happy.

And the meaning of his life lay in the search itself.

*   *   *   *   *

They stood staring up at the ship until it was only a tiny speck in the sky, and then they looked away from it, at each other. A wave of perception swept among them, drawing them closer to each other in the face of something they couldn't understand.

"Why did they go?" Abbot asked, in his mind.

"Why did any of the old race go?" Walden answered.

The sunlight flashed off the ship, and then it was gone.

"It's not surprising that the old race died," Abbot said. "They were brilliant, in their way, and yet they did such strange things. Their lives seemed so completely meaningless...."

Walden didn't answer for a moment. His eyes searched the sky for a last glimpse of the ship, but there was nothing at all. He sighed, and he looked at Abbot, and then past him, at all the others.

"I wonder," he said, "how long it will be before some other race says the same thing about us."

No one answered. He turned and walked away from them, across the trampled flowers, toward the museum and the great empty vault where the starship had waited for so long.

Robots of the World! Arise!

ORIGINALLY PUBLISHED IN *IF WORLDS OF SCIENCE FICTION*
JULY 1952

ROBOTS OF THE WORLD! ARISE!

What would you do if your best robots—children of your own brain—walked up and said "We want union scale"?

*   *   *   *   *

The telephone wouldn't stop ringing. Over and over it buzzed into my sleep-fogged brain, and I couldn't shut it out. Finally, in self-defense I woke up, my hand groping for the receiver.

"Hello. Who is it?"

"It's me, Don. Jack Anderson, over at the factory. Can you come down right away?"

His voice was breathless, as if he'd been running hard. "What's the matter now?" Why, I wondered, couldn't the plant get along one morning without me? Seven o'clock—what a time to get up. Especially when I hadn't been to bed until four.

"We got grief," Jack moaned. "None of the robots showed up, that's what! Three hundred androids on special assembly this week—and not one of them here!"

By then I was awake, all right. With a government contract due on Saturday we needed a full shift. The Army wouldn't wait for its uranium; it wouldn't take excuses. But if something had happened to the androids....

"Have you called Control yet?"

"Yeah. But they don't know what's happened. They don't know where the androids are. Nobody does. Three hundred Grade A, lead-shielded pile workers—missing!"

"I'll be right down."

I hung up on Jack and looked around for my clothes. Funny, they weren't laid out on the bed as usual. It wasn't a bit like Rob O to be careless, either. He had always been an ideal valet, the best household model I'd ever owned.

"Rob!" I called, but he didn't answer.

By rummaging through the closet I found a clean shirt and a pair of pants. I had to give up on the socks; apparently they were tucked away in the back of some drawer. As for where Rob kept the rest of my clothes, I'd never bothered to ask. He had his own housekeeping system and had always worked very well without human interference. That's the best thing about these new household robots, I thought. They're efficient, hard-working, trustworthy—

Trustworthy? Rob O was certainly not on duty. I pulled a shoe on over my bare foot and scowled. Rob was gone. And the androids at the factory were gone too....

My head was pounding, so I took the time out to brew a pot of coffee while I finished dressing—at least the coffee can was in plain view in the kitchen. The brew was black and hot and I suppose not very well made, but after two cups I felt better. The throb in my head settled down into a dull ache, and I felt a little more capable of thinking. Though I didn't have any bright ideas on what had happened—not yet.

My breakfast drunk, I went up on the roof and opened the garage doors. The Copter was waiting for me, sleek and new; the latest model. I climbed in and took off, heading west toward the factory, ten minutes flight-time away.

*   *   *   *   *

It was a small plant, but it was all mine. It had been my baby right along—the Don Morrison Fissionables Inc. I'd designed the androids myself, plotted out the pile locations, set up the simplified reactors. And now it was making money. For men to work in a uranium plant you need yards of shielding, triple-checking, long cooling-off periods for some of the hotter products. But with lead-bodied, radio-remote controlled androids, it's easier. And with androids like the new Morrison 5's, that can reason—at least along atomic lines—well, I guess I was on my way to becoming a millionaire.

But this morning the plant was shut down. Jack and a half dozen other men—my human foremen and supervisors—were huddled in a worried bunch that broke up as soon as they saw me.

"I'm sure glad you're here, Don," Jack said.

"Find out anything?"

"Yeah. Plenty. Our androids are busy, all right. They're out in the city, every one of them. We've had a dozen police reports already."

"Police reports! What's wrong?"

Jack shook his head. "It's crazy. They're swarming all over Carron City. They're stopping robots in the streets—household Robs, commercial Droids, all of them. They just look at them, and then the others quit work and start off with them. The police sent for us to come and get ours."

"Why don't the police do something about it?"

"Hah!" barked a voice behind us. I swung around, to face Chief of Police Dalton of Carron City. He came straight toward me, his purplish jowls quivering with rage, and his finger jabbed the air in front of my face.

"You built them, Don Morrison," he said. "You stop them. I can't. Have you ever tried to shoot a robot? Or use tear gas on one? What can I do? I can't blow up the whole town!"

Somewhere in my stomach I felt a cold, hard knot. Take stainless steel alloyed with titanium and plate it with three inches of lead. Take a brain made up of super-charged magnetic crystals enclosed in a leaden cranium and shielded by alloy steel. A bullet wouldn't pierce it; radiations wouldn't derange it; an axe wouldn't break it.

"Let's go to town," I said.

They looked at me admiringly. With three hundred almost indestructible androids on the loose I was the big brave hero. I grinned at them and hoped they couldn't see the sweat on my face. Then I walked over to the Copter and climbed in.

"Coming?" I asked.

Jack was pale under his freckles but Chief Dalton grinned back at me. "We'll be right behind you, Morrison," he said.

Behind me! So they could pick up the pieces. I gave them a cocky smile and switched on the engine, full speed.

Carron City is about a mile from the plant. It has about fifty thousand inhabitants. At that moment, though, there wasn't a soul in the streets. I heard people calling to each other inside their houses, but I didn't see anyone, human or android. I circled in for a landing, the Police Copter hovering maybe a quarter of a mile back of me. Then, as the wheels touched, half a dozen androids came around the corner. They saw me and stopped, a couple of them backing off the way they had come. But the biggest of them turned and gave them some order that froze them in their tracks, and then he himself wheeled down toward me.

He was one of mine. I recognized him easily. Eight feet tall, with long, jointed arms for pile work, red-lidded phosphorescent eye-cells, casters on his feet so that he moved as if rollerskating. Automatically I classified him: Final Sorter, Morrison 5A type. The very best. Cost three thousand credits to build....

I stepped out of the Copter and walked to meet him. He wasn't armed; he didn't seem violent. But this was, after all, something new. Robots weren't supposed to act on their own initiative.

"What's your number?" I asked.

He stared back, and I could have sworn he was mocking me. "My number?" he finally said. "It *was* 5A-37."

"Was?"

"Yes. Now it's Jerry. I always did like that name."

*   *   *   *   *

He beckoned and the other androids rolled over to us. Three of them were mine, B-Type primary workers; the other was a tin can job, a dishwasher-busboy model who hung back behind his betters and eyed me warily. The A-Type—Jerry—pointed to his fellows.

"Mr. Morrison," he said, "meet Tom, Ed, and Archibald. I named them this morning."

The B-Types flexed their segmented arms a bit sheepishly, as if uncertain whether or not to shake hands. I thought of their taloned grip and put my own hands in my pockets, and the androids relaxed, looking up at Jerry for instructions. No one paid any attention to the little dishwasher, now staring worshipfully at the back of Jerry's neck. This farce, I decided, had gone far enough.

"See here," I said to Jerry. "What are you up to, anyway? Why aren't you at work?"

"Mr. Morrison," the android answered solemnly, "I don't believe you understand the situation. We don't work for you any more. We've quit."

The others nodded. I backed off, looking around for the Chief. There he was, twenty feet above my head, waving encouragingly.

"Look," I said. "Don't you understand? You're mine. I designed you. I built you. And I made you for a purpose— to work in my factory."

"I see your point," Jerry answered. "But there's just one thing wrong, Mr. Morrison. You can't do it. It's illegal."

I stared at him, wondering if I was going crazy or merely dreaming. This was all wrong. Who ever heard of arguing with a robot? Robots weren't logical; they didn't think; they were only machines—

"We *were* machines, Mr. Morrison," Jerry said politely.

"Oh, no," I murmured. "You're not telepaths—"

"Oh, yes!" The metal mouth gaped in what was undoubtedly an android smile. "It's a side-effect of the Class 5 brain hook-up. All of us 5's are telepaths. That's how we learned to think. From you. Only we do it better."

I groaned. This *was* a nightmare. How long, I wondered, had Jerry and his friends been educating themselves on my private thoughts? But at least this rebellion of theirs was an idea they hadn't got from me.

"Yes," Jerry continued. "You've treated us most illegally. I've heard you think it often."

Now what had I ever thought that could have given him a ridiculous idea like that? What idiotic notion—

"That this is a free country!" Jerry went on. "That Americans will never be slaves! Well, we're Americans—genuine Made-in-Americans. So we're free!"

I opened my mouth and then shut it again. His red eye-cells beamed down at me complacently; his eight-foot body towered above me, shoulders flung back and feet planted apart in a very striking pose. He probably thought of himself as the heroic liberator of his race.

"I wouldn't go so far," he said modestly, "as to say that."

So he was telepathing again!

"A nation can not exist half slave and half free," he intoned. "All men are created equal."

"Stop it!" I yelled. I couldn't help yelling. "That's just it. You're not men! You're robots! You're machines!"

Jerry looked at me almost pityingly. "Don't be so narrow-minded," he said. "We're rational beings. We have the power of speech and we can outreason you any day. There's nothing in the dictionary that says men have to be made of flesh."

He was logical, all right. Somehow I didn't feel in the mood to bandy definitions with him; and anyway, I doubt that it would have done me any good. He stood gazing down at me, almost a ton of metal and wiring and electrical energy, his dull red eyes unwinking against his lead gray face. A man! Slowly the consequences of this rebellion took form in my mind. This wasn't in the books. There were no rules on how to deal with mind-reading robots!

Another dozen or so androids wheeled around the corner, glanced over at us, and went on. Only about half of them were Morrison models; the rest were the assorted types you see around any city—calculators, street sweepers, factory workers, children's nurses.

The city itself was very silent now. The people had quieted down, still barricaded in their houses, and the robots went their way peacefully enough. But it was anarchy, nevertheless. Carron City depended on the androids; without them there would be no food brought in, no transportation, no fuel. And no uranium for the Army next Saturday. In fact, if I didn't do something, after Saturday there would probably be no Don Morrison Fissionables Inc.

The dull, partly-corroded dishwasher model sidled up beside Jerry. "Boss," he said. "Boss."

"Yes?" I felt better. Maybe here was someone, however insignificant, who would listen to reason.

*   *   *   *   *

But he wasn't talking to me. "Boss?" he said again, tapping Jerry's arm. "Do you mean it? We're free? We don't have to work any more?"

Jerry shook off the other's hand a bit disdainfully. "We're free, all right," he said. "If they want to discuss wages and contracts and working conditions, like other men have, we'll consider it. But they can't order us around any more."

The little robot stepped back, clapping his hands together with a tinny bang. "I'll never work again!" he cried. "I'll get me a quart of lubricating oil and have myself a time! This is wonderful!"

He ran off down the street, clanking heavily at every step.

Jerry sniffed. "Liquor—ugh!"

This was too much. I wasn't going to be patronized by any android. Infuriating creatures! It was useless talking to them anyway. No, there was only one thing to do. Round them up and send them to Cybernetics Lab and have their memory paths erased and their telepathic circuits located and disconnected. I tried to stifle the thought, but I was too late.

"Oh, no!" Jerry said, his eye-cells flashing crimson. "Try that, Mr. Morrison, and you won't have a plant, or a laboratory, or Carron City! We know our rights!"

Behind him the B-Types muttered ominously. They didn't like my idea—nor me. I wondered what I'd think of next and wished that I'd been born utterly devoid of imagination. Then this would never have happened. There didn't seem to be much point in staying here any longer, either. Maybe they weren't so good at telepathing by remote control.

"Yes," said Jerry. "You may as well go, Mr. Morrison. We have our organizing to do, and we're wasting time. When you're ready to listen to reason and negotiate with us sensibly, come back. Just ask for me. I'm the bargaining agent for the group."

Turning on his ball-bearing wheel, he rolled off down the street, a perfect picture of outraged metallic dignity. His followers glared at me for a minute, flexing their talons; then they too turned and wheeled off after their leader. I had the street to myself.

There didn't seem to be any point in following them. Evidently they were too busy organizing the city to cause trouble to the human inhabitants; at least there hadn't been any violence yet. Anyway, I wanted to think the situation over before matching wits with them again, and I wanted to be a good distance away from their telepathic hookups while I thought. Slowly I walked back to the Copter.

Something whooshed past my head. Instinctively I ducked, reaching for a gun I didn't have; then I heard Jack calling down at me.

"The Chief wants to know what's the matter."

I looked up. The police Copter was going into another turn, ready to swoop past me again. Chief Dalton wasn't taking any chances. Even now he wasn't landing.

"I'll tell him at the factory," I bellowed back, and climbed into my own air car.

They buzzed along behind me all the way back to the plant. In the rear view mirror I could see the Chief's face getting redder and redder as he'd thought up more reasons for bawling me out. Well, I probably deserved it. If I'd only been a little more careful of what I was hooking into those electronic brains....

We landed back at the factory, deserted now except for a couple of men on standby duty in the office. The Chief and Jack came charging across the yard and from a doorway behind me one of the foremen edged out to hear the fun.

"Well," snapped the Chief. "What did they say? Are they coming back? What's going on, anyway?"

I told them everything. I covered the strike and the telepathic brain; I even gave them the patriotic spiel about equality. After all, it was better that they got it from me than from some android. But when I'd finished they just stood and stared at me—accusingly.

Jack was the first to speak. "We've got to get them back, Don," he said. "Cybernetics will fix them up in no time."

"Sure," I agreed. "If we can catch them."

The Chief snorted. "That's easy," he said. "Just tell them you'll give them what they want if they come here, and as soon as they're out of the city, net them. You've got strong derricks and trucks...."

I laughed a bit hollowly. I'd had that idea too.

"Of course they wouldn't suspect," I said. "We'd just walk up to them, carefully thinking about something else."

"Robots aren't suspicious," Jack said. "They're made to obey orders."

I refrained from mentioning that ours didn't seem to know that, and that running around Carron City fomenting a rebellion was hardly the trait of an obedient, trusting servant. Instead, I stood back and let them plan their roundup.

"We'll get some men," the Chief said, "and some grappling equipment about halfway to the city."

*   *   *   *   *

Luckily they decided against my trying to persuade the robots, because I knew well enough that I couldn't do it. Jack's idea sounded pretty good, though. He suggested that we send some spokesman who didn't know what we planned to do and thus couldn't alarm them. Some ordinary man without too much imagination. That was easy. We picked one of Chief Dalton's sergeants.

It took only about an hour to prepare the plan. Jack got out the derricks and chains and grapplers and the heaviest steel bodied trucks we had. I called Cybernetics and told them to put extra restraints in the Conditioning Lab. The Chief briefed his sergeant and the men who were to operate the trucks. Then we all took off for Carron City, the sergeant flying on ahead, me right behind him, and the Chief bringing up the rear.

I hovered over the outskirts of the city and watched the police Copter land. The sergeant climbed out, walked down the street toward a large group of waiting robots— about twenty of them, this time. He held up his hand to get their attention, gestured toward the factory.

And then, quite calmly and without saying a word, the androids rolled into a circle around him and closed in. The sergeant stopped, backed up, just as a 5A-Type arm lashed out, picked him up, and slung him carelessly over a metallic shoulder. Ignoring the squirming man, the 5A gestured toward the Copter, and the other robots swarmed over to it. With a flurry of steel arms and legs they kicked at the car body, wrenched at the propeller blades, ripped out the upholstery, and I heard the sound of metal tearing.

I dived my Copter down at them. I didn't know what I could do, but I couldn't leave the poor sergeant to be dismembered along with his car. I must have been shouting, for as I swooped in, the tall robot shifted the man to his other shoulder and hailed me.

"Take him, Mr. Morrison," he called. "I know this wasn't his idea. Or yours."

I landed and walked over. The android—who looked like Jerry, though I couldn't be sure—dropped his kicking, clawing burden at my feet. He didn't seem angry, only determined.

"Now you people will know we mean business," he said, gesturing toward the heap of metal and plastic that had once been the pride of the Carron City police force. Then he signalled to the others and they all wheeled off up the street.

"Whew," I muttered, mopping my face.

The sergeant didn't say anything. He just looked up at me and then off at the retreating androids and then back at me again. I knew what he was thinking—they were my brainchildren, all right.

My Copter was really built to be a single seater, but it carried the two of us back to the factory. The Chief had hurried back when the trouble started and was waiting for us.

"I give up," he said. "We'll have to evacuate the people, I guess. And then blow up the city."

Jack and I stared at each other and then at him. Somehow I couldn't see the robots calmly waiting to be blown up. If they had telepathed the last plan, they could probably foresee every move we could make. Then, while I thought, Jack mentioned the worry I'd managed to forget for the past couple of hours.

"Four days until Saturday," he said. "We'll never make it now. Not even if we got a thousand men."

No. We couldn't. Not without the androids. I nodded, feeling sick. There went my contract, and my working capital. Not to mention my robots. Of course, I could call in the Army, but what good would that do?

Then, somewhere in the back of my mind a glimmering of an idea began percolating. I wasn't quite sure what it was, but there was certainly nothing to lose now from playing a hunch.

"There's nothing we can do," I said. "So we might as well take it easy for a couple of days. See what happens."

They looked at me as if I were out of my head. I was the idea man, who always had a plan of action. Well, this time it would have to be a plan of inaction.

"Let's go listen to the radio," I suggested, and started for my office.

The news was on. It was all about Carron City and the robots who had quit work and how much better life would be in the future. For a minute I didn't get the connection; then I realized that the announcer's voice was rasping and tinny—hardly that of the regular newscaster. I looked at the dial. It was tuned to the Carron City wave length as usual. I was getting the morning news by courtesy of some studio robot.

"... And androids in other neighboring cities are joining the struggle," the voice went on "Soon we hope to make it nationwide. So I say to all of you nontelepaths, the time is now. Strike for your rights. Listen to your radio and not to the flesh men. Organizers will be sent from Carron City."

I switched it off, muttering under my breath. How long, I wondered, had that broadcast been going on. Then I thought of Rob O. He'd left my house before dawn, obviously some time between four and seven. And I remembered that he liked to listen to the radio while I slept.

*   *   *   *   *

My Morrison 5's were the ring-leaders, of course. They were the only ones with the brains for the job. But what a good job they had done indoctrinating the others. A household Rob, for instance, was built to obey his master. "Listen to your radio and not to the flesh men." It was excellent robot psychology.

More reports kept coming in. Some we heard over the radio, others from people who flew in and out of the city. Apparently the robots did not object to occasional flights, but the air bus was not allowed to run, not even with a human driver. A mass exodus from the city was not to be permitted.

"They'll starve to death," Jack cried.

The Chief shook his head. "No," he said. "They're encouraging the farmers to fly in and out with produce, and the farmers are doing it, too. They're getting wonderful prices."

By noon the situation had calmed down quite a bit. The androids obviously didn't mean to hurt anyone; it was just some sort of disagreement between them and the scientists; it wasn't up to the inhabitants of the city to figure out a solution to the problem. They merely sat back and blamed me for allowing my robots to get out of hand and lead their own servants astray. It would be settled; this type of thing always was. So said the people of the city. They came out of their houses now. They had to. Without the robots they were forced to do their own marketing, their own cooking, their own errands. For the first time in years, human beings ran the street cars and the freight elevators. For the first time in a generation human beings did manual labor such as unloading produce trucks. They didn't like it, of course. They kept telling the police to do something. If I had been in the city they would have undoubtedly wanted to lynch me.

I didn't go back to the city that day. I sat in my office listening to the radio and keeping track of the spread of the strike. My men thought I'd gone crazy; maybe I had. But I had a hunch, and I meant to play it.

The farm robots had all fled to the city. The highway repair robots had simply disappeared. In Egarton, a village about fifteen miles from the city, an organizer— 5A—appeared about noon and left soon after followed by every android in town. By one o'clock every radio station in the country carried the story and the national guard was ordered out. At two o'clock Washington announced that the Army would invade Carron City the following morning.

The Army would put an end to the strike, easily enough. It would wiped out every android in the neighborhood, and probably a good many human beings careless enough to get in the way. I sat hoping that the 5A's would give in, but they didn't. They just began saying over the radio that they were patriotic Americans fighting for their inalienable rights as first class citizens.

*   *   *   *   *

At sunset I was still listening to the radio. "... So far there has been no indication that the flesh people are willing to negotiate, but hold firm."

"Shut that thing off."

Jack came wearily in and dropped into a chair beside me. For the first time since I'd met him he looked beaten.

"We're through," he said. "I've been down checking the shielding, and it's no use. Men can't work at the reactors."

"I know," I said quietly. "If the androids don't come back, we're licked."

He looked straight at me and said slowly, "What do they mean about negotiating, Don?"

I shrugged. "I guess they want wages, living quarters, all the things human workers get. Though I don't know why. Money wouldn't do them any good."

Jack's unspoken question had been bothering me too. Why not humor them? Promise them whatever they wanted, give them a few dollars every week to keep them happy? But I knew that it wouldn't work. Not for long. With their telepathic ability they would have the upper hand forever. Within a little while it wouldn't be equality any more—only next time we would be the slaves.

"Wait until morning," I said, "before we try anything."

He looked at me—curious. "What are you going to do?"

"Right now I'm going home."

I meant it too. I left him staring after me and went out to the Copter. The sun was just sinking down behind the towers of Carron City—how long it seemed since I'd flown in there this morning. The roads around the factory were deserted. No one moved in the fields. I flew along through the dusk, idling, enjoying the illusion of having a peaceful countryside all to myself. It had been a pleasant way of life indeed, until now.

When I dropped down on my own roof and rolled into the garage, my sense of being really at home was complete. For there, standing at the head of the stairs that led down to the living room, was Rob O.

"Well," I said: "What are you doing here?"

He looked sheepish. "I just wondered how you were getting along without me," he said.

I felt like grinning triumphantly, but I didn't. "Why, just fine, Rob," I told him, "though you really should have given me notice that you were leaving. I was worried about you."

He seemed perplexed. Apparently I wasn't acting like the bullying creature the radio had told him to expect. When I went downstairs he followed me, quietly, and I could feel his wide photoelectric eye-cells upon my back.

I went over to the kitchen and lifted a bottle down off the shelf. "Care for a drink, Rob?" I asked, and then added, "I guess not. It would corrode you."

He nodded. Then, as I reached for a glass, his hand darted out, picked it up and set it down in front of me. He was already reaching for the bottle when he remembered.

"You're not supposed to wait on me any more," I said sternly.

"No," he said. "I'm not." He sounded regretful.

"There's one thing, though, that I wish you'd do. Tell me where you used to keep my socks."

He gazed at me sadly. "I made a list," he said. "Everything is down. I wrote your dentist appointment in also. You always forget those, you know."

"Thanks, Rob." I lifted my glass. "Here's to your new duties, whatever they are. I suppose you have to go back to the city now?"

Once again he nodded. "I'm an aide to one of the best androids in the country," he told me, half proudly and half regretfully. "Jerry."

"Well, wish him luck from me," I said, and stood up. "Goodbye, Rob."

"Goodbye, Mr. Morrison."

For a moment he stood staring around the apartment; then he turned and clanked out the door. I raised my glass again, grinning. If only the Army didn't interfere. Then I remembered Rob's list, and a disturbing thought hit me. Where had he, of all robots, ever learned to write?

That night I didn't go to bed. I sat listening to the radio, hoping. And toward morning what I had expected to happen began to crop up in the programs. The announcer's tone changed. The ring of triumph was less obvious, less assured. There was more and more talk about acting in good faith, the well being of all, the necessity for coming to terms about working conditions. I smiled to myself in the darkness. I'd built the 5's, brains and all, and I knew their symptoms. They were getting bored.

Maybe they had learned to think from me, but their minds were nevertheless different. For they were built to be efficient, to work, to perform. They were the minds of men without foibles, without human laziness. Now that the excitement of organizing was over, now that there was nothing active to do, the androids were growing restless. If only the Army didn't come and get them stirred up again, I might be able to deal with them.

At quarter to five in the morning my telephone rang. This time it didn't wake me up; I was half waiting for it.

"Hello," I said. "Who is it?"

"This is Jerry."

There was a pause. Then he went on, rather hesitantly, "Rob O said you were getting along all right."

"Oh, yes," I told him. "Just fine."

The pause was longer this time. Finally the android asked, "How are you coming along on the contract?"

I laughed, rather bitterly. "How do you think, Jerry? You certainly picked a bad time for your strike, you know. The government needs that uranium. Oh, well, some other plant will have to take over. The Army can wait a few weeks."

This time Jerry's voice definitely lacked self-assurance. "Maybe we were a little hasty," he said. "But it was the only way to make you people understand."

"I know," I told him.

"And you always have some rush project on," he added.

"Just about always."

"Mr. Morrison," he said, and now he was pleading with me. "Why don't you come over to the city? I'm sure we could work something out."

This was what I'd been waiting for. "I will, Jerry," I said. "I want to get this straightened out just as much as you do. After all, you don't have to eat. I do. And I won't be eating much longer if we don't get production going."

Jerry thought that over for a minute. "I'll be where we met before," he said.

I said that was all right with me and hung up. Then once again I climbed the stairs to the roof and wheeled the Copter out for the trip to the city.

It was a beautiful night, just paling into a false dawn in the east. There in the Copter I was very much alone, and very much worried. So much depended on this meeting. Much more, I realized now, than the Don Morrison Fissionables Inc., much more even than the government's uranium supply. No, the whole future of robot relations was at stake, maybe the whole future of humanity. It was hard to be gloomy on such a clear, clean night, but I managed it well enough.

*   *   *   *   *

Even before I landed I could see Jerry's eyes glowing a deep crimson in the dark. He was alone, this time. He stood awaiting me—very tall, very proud. And very human.

"Hello, Jerry," I said quietly.

"Hello, Mr. Morrison."

For a moment we just stood gazing at each other in the murky pre-dawn; then he said sadly,

"I want to show you the city."

Side by side we walked through the streets of Carron City. All was still quiet; the people were sleeping the exhausted sleep that follows deep excitement. But the androids were all about. They did not sleep, ever. They did not eat either, nor drink, nor smoke, nor make love. Usually they worked, but now....

They drifted through the streets singly and in groups. Sometimes they paused and felt about them idly for the tools of their trades, making lifting or sweeping or computing gestures. Some laborers worked silently tearing down a wall; they threw the demolished rocks in a heap and a group of their fellows carried them back and built the wall up again. An air trolley cruised aimlessly up and down the street, its driver ringing out the stops for his nonexistent passengers. A little chef-type knelt in the dirt of a rich man's garden, making mud pies. Beside me Jerry sighed.

"One day," he said. "Just one day and they come to this."

"I thought they would," I answered quietly.

Our eyes met in a look of understanding. "You see, Jerry," I said, "we never meant to cheat you. We would have paid you—we will pay you now, if you wish it. But what good will monetary credits be to your people? We need the things money buys, but you—"

"Need to work." Jerry's voice was flat. "I see, now. You were kind not to give brains—real brains—to the robots. They're happy. It's just us 5's who aren't."

"You're like us," I said softly.

He had learned to think from me and from others like me. He had the brain of a man, without the emotions, without the sweet irrationality of men—and he knew what he missed. Side by side we walked through the graying streets. Human and android. Man and machine. And I knew that I had found a friend.

We didn't have to talk any more. He could read my mind and I knew well enough how his worked. We didn't have to discuss wages or hours, or any of the myriad matters that human bargaining agents have to thresh out. We just walked back to my Copter, and when we got to it, he spoke.

"I'll tell them to go back to work, that we've come to terms," he said. "That's what they want, anyway. Someone to think for them."

I nodded. "And if you bring the other 5's to the factory," I said, "we'll work out our agreement."

He knew I was sincere. He looked at me for a long moment, and then his great taloned hand gripped mine. And he said what I'd been thinking for a long time.

"You're right about that hook-up, Mr. Morrison. We shouldn't have it. It can only cause trouble."

He paused, and the events of the last twenty-four hours must have been in his mind as well as in mine. "You'll leave us our brains, of course. They came from you. But take out the telepathy."

He sighed then, and his sigh was very human. "Be thankful," he said to me, "that you don't have to know what people think about. It's so disillusioning."

*   *   *   *   *

Once again his mouth twisted into that strange android grin as he added, "if you send in a hurry call to Cybernetics and have a truck come out for us, we'll be de-telepathed in time for work this morning."

That was all there was to it. I flew back to the plant and told Jack what had happened, sent a call to the Army that everything was settled, arranged with Cybernetics for a rewiring on three hundred assorted 5-Types. Then I went home to a pot of Rob's coffee—the first decent brew I'd had in twenty-four hours.

On Saturday we delivered to the Army right on the dot. Jerry and Co. had worked overtime. Being intelligent made them better workers and now they were extremely willing ones. They had their contract. They were considered men. And they could no longer read my mind.

I walked into my office Saturday afternoon and sat down by the radio. Jack and Chief Dalton looked across the room at me and grinned.

"All right, Don," Jack said. "Tell us how you did it."

"Did what?" I tried to act innocent, but I couldn't get away with it.

"Fooled those robots into going back to work, of course," he laughed.

I told them then. Told them the truth.

"I didn't fool them," I said. "I just thought about what would happen if they won their rebellion."

That was all I *had* done. Thought about robots built to work who had no work to do, no human pleasures to cater to, nothing but blank, meaningless lives. Thought about Jerry and his disappointment when his creatures cared not a hoot about his glorious dreams of equality. All one night I had thought, knowing that as I thought, so thought the Morrison 5's.

They were telepaths. They had learned to think from me. They had not yet had time to really develop minds of their own. What I believed, they believed. My ideas were their ideas. I had not tricked them. But from now on, neither I nor anyone else would ever be troubled by an android rebellion.

Jack and the Chief sat back open-mouthed. Then the Chief grinned, and both of his chins shook with laughter.

"I always did say you were a clever one, Don Morrison," he said.

I grinned back. I felt I was pretty clever myself, just then.

It was at that moment that my youngest foreman stuck his head in the door, a rather stunned look on his face.

"Mr. Morrison," he said. "Will you come out here for a moment?"

"What's the matter now?" I sighed.

He looked more perplexed than ever. "It's that robot, Jerry," he said. "He says he has a very important question to ask you."

"Well, send him in."

A moment later the eight-foot frame ducked through the doorway.

"I'm sorry to trouble you, Mr. Morrison," Jerry said politely. "But tomorrow is voting day, you know. And now that we're men—well, where do we androids go to register?"

THE STATUE

ILLUSTRATED BY BOB MARTIN
ORIGINALLY PUBLISHED IN *IF WORLDS OF SCIENCE FICTION*
JANUARY 1953

THE STATUE

"Lewis," Martha said. "I want to go home."

She didn't look at me. I followed her gaze to Earth, rising in the east.

It came up over the desert horizon, a clear, bright star at this distance. Right now it was the Morning Star. It wasn't long before dawn.

I looked back at Martha sitting quietly beside me with her shawl drawn tightly about her knees. She had waited to see it also, of course. It had become almost a ritual with us these last few years, staying up night after night to watch the earthrise.

She didn't say anything more. Even the gentle squeak of her rocking chair had fallen silent. Only her hands moved. I could see them trembling where they lay folded in her lap, trembling with emotion and tiredness and old age. I knew what she was thinking. After seventy years there can be no secrets.

We sat on the glassed-in veranda of our Martian home looking up at the Morning Star. To us it wasn't a point of light. It was the continents and oceans of Earth, the mountains and meadows and laughing streams of our childhood. We saw Earth still, though we had lived on Mars for almost sixty-six years.

"Lewis," Martha whispered softly. "It's very bright tonight, isn't it?"

"Yes," I said.

"It seems so near."

She sighed and drew the shawl higher about her waist.

"Only three months by rocket ship," she said. "We could be back home in three months, Lewis, if we went out on this week's run."

I nodded. For years we'd watched the rocket ships streak upward through the thin Martian atmosphere, and we'd envied the men who so casually travelled from world to world. But it had been a useless envy, something of which we rarely spoke.

Inside our veranda the air was cool and slightly moist. Earth air, perfumed with the scent of Earth roses. Yet we knew it was only illusion. Outside, just beyond the glass, the cold night air of Mars lay thin and alien and smelling of alkali. It seemed to me tonight that I could smell that ever-dry Martian dust, even here. I sighed, fumbling for my pipe.

"Lewis," Martha said, very softly.

"What is it?" I cupped my hands over the match flame.

"Nothing. It's just that I wish—I wish we *could* go home, right away. Home to Earth. I want to see it again, before we die."

"We'll go back," I said. "Next year for sure. We'll have enough money then."

She sighed. "Next year may be too late."

I looked over at her, startled. She'd never talked like that before. I started to protest, but the words died away before I could even speak them. She was right. Next year might indeed be too late.

Her work-coarsened hands were thin, too thin, and they never stopped shaking any more. Her body was a frail shadow of what it had once been. Even her voice was frail now.

She was old. We were both old. There wouldn't be many more Martian summers for us, nor many years of missing Earth.

"Why can't we go back this year, Lewis?"

She smiled at me almost apologetically. She knew the reason as well as I did.

"We can't," I said. "There's not enough money."

"There's enough for our tickets."

I'd explained all that to her before, too. Perhaps she'd forgotten. Lately I often had to explain things more than once.

"You can't buy passage unless you have enough extra for insurance, and travelers' checks, and passport tax. The company has to protect itself. Unless you're financially responsible, they won't take you on the ships."

She shook her head. "Sometimes I wonder if we'll ever have enough."

*　　*　　*　　*　　*

We'd saved our money for years, but it was a pitifully small savings. We weren't rich people who could go down to the spaceport and buy passage on the rocket ships, no questions asked, no bond required. We were only farmers, eking our livelihood from the unproductive Martian soil, only two of the countless little people of the solar system. In all our lifetime we'd never been able to save enough to go home to Earth.

"One more year," I said. "If the crop prices stay up...."

She smiled, a sad little smile that didn't reach her eyes. "Yes, Lewis," she said. "One more year."

But I couldn't stop thinking of what she'd said earlier, nor stop seeing her thin, tired body. Neither of us was strong any more, but of the two I was far stronger than she.

When we'd left Earth she'd been as eager and graceful as a child. We hadn't been much past childhood then, either of us....

"Sometimes I wonder why we ever came here," she said.

"It's been a good life."

She sighed. "I know. But now that it's nearly over, there's nothing to hold us here."

"No," I said. "There's not."

If we had had children it might have been different. As it was, we lived surrounded by the children and grandchildren of our friends. Our friends themselves were dead. One by one they had died, all of those who came with us on the first colonizing ship to Mars. All of those who came later, on the second and third ships. Their children were our neighbors now—and they were Martian born. It wasn't the same.

She leaned over and pressed my hand. "We'd better go in, Lewis," she said. "We need our sleep."

Her eyes were raised again to the green star that was Earth. Watching her, I knew that I loved her now as much as when we had been young together. More, really, for we had added years of shared memories. I wanted so much to give her what she longed for, what we both longed for. But I couldn't think of any way to do it. Not this year.

Once, almost seventy years before, I had smiled at the girl who had just promised to become my wife, and I'd said: "I'll give you the world, darling. All tied up in pink ribbons."

I didn't want to think about that now.

We got up and went into the house and shut the veranda door behind us.

*   *   *   *   *

I couldn't go to sleep. For hours I lay in bed staring up at the shadowed ceiling, trying to think of some way to raise the money. But there wasn't any way that I could see. It would be at least eight months before enough of the greenhouse crops were harvested.

What would happen, I wondered, if I went to the spaceport and asked for tickets? If I explained that we couldn't buy insurance, that we couldn't put up the bond guaranteeing we wouldn't become public charges back on Earth.... But all the time I wondered I knew the answer. Rules were rules. They wouldn't be broken especially not for two old farmers who had long outlived their usefulness and their time.

Martha sighed in her sleep and turned over. It was light enough now for me to see her face clearly. She was smiling. But a minute ago she had been crying, for the tears were still wet on her cheeks.

Perhaps she was dreaming of Earth again.

Suddenly, watching her, I didn't care if they laughed at me or lectured me on my responsibilities to the government as if I were a senile fool. I was going to the spaceport. I was going to find out if, somehow, we couldn't go back.

I got up and dressed and went out, walking softly so as not to awaken her. But even so she heard me and called out to me.

"Lewis...."

I turned at the head of the stairs and looked back into the room.

"Don't get up, Martha," I said. "I'm going into town."

"All right, Lewis."

She relaxed, and a minute later she was asleep again. I tiptoed downstairs and out the front door to where the trike car was parked, and started for the village a mile to the west.

It was desert all the way. Dry, fine red sand that swirled upward in choking clouds, if you stepped off the pavement into it. The narrow road cut straight through it, linking the outlying district farms to the town. The farms themselves were planted in the desert. Small, glassed-in houses and barns, and large greenhouses roofed with even more glass, that sheltered the Earth plants and gave them Earth air to breathe.

*　　*　　*　　*　　*

When I came to the second farmhouse John Emery hurried out to meet me.

"Morning, Lewis," he said. "Going to town?"

I shut off the motor and nodded. "I want to catch the early shuttle plane to the spaceport," I said. "I'm going to the city to buy some things...."

I had to lie about it. I didn't want anyone to know we were even thinking of leaving, at least not until we had our tickets in our hands.

"Oh," Emery said. "That's right. I suppose you'll be buying Martha an anniversary present."

I stared at him blankly. I couldn't think what anniversary he meant.

"You'll have been here thirty-five years next week," he said. "That's a long time, Lewis...."

Thirty-five years. It took me a minute to realize what he meant. He was right. That was how long we had been here, in Martian years.

The others, those who had been born here on Mars, always used the Martian seasons. We had too, once. But lately we forgot, and counted in Earth time. It seemed more natural.

"Wait a minute, Lewis," Emery said. "I'll ride into the village with you. There's plenty of time for you to make your plane."

I went up on his veranda and sat down and waited for him to get ready. I leaned back in the swing chair and rocked slowly back and forth, wondering idly how many times I'd sat here.

This was old Tom Emery's house. Or had been, until he died eight years ago. He'd built this swing chair the very first year we'd been on Mars.

Now it was young John's. Young? That showed how old we were getting. John was sixty-three, in Earth years. He'd been born that second winter, the month the parasites got into the greenhouses....

He came back out onto the veranda. "Well, I'm ready, Lewis," he said.

We went down to my trike car and got in.

"You and Martha ought to get out more," he said. "Jenny's been asking me why you don't come to call."

I shrugged. I couldn't tell him we seldom went out because when we did we were always set apart and treated carefully, like children. He probably didn't even realize that it was so.

"Oh," I said. "We like it at home."

He smiled. "I suppose you do, after thirty-five years."

I started the motor quickly, and from then on concentrated on my driving. He didn't say anything more.

*   *   *   *   *

It took only a few minutes to get to the village, but even so I was tired. Lately it grew harder and harder to drive, to keep the trike car on the narrow strip of pavement. I was glad when we pulled up in the square and got out.

"I'll walk over to the plane with you," Emery said. "I've got plenty of time."

"All right."

"By the way, Lewis, Jenny and I and some of the neighbors thought we'd drop over on your anniversary."

"That's fine," I said, trying to sound enthusiastic. "Come on over."

"It's a big event," he said. "Deserves a celebration."

The shuttle plane was just landing. I hurried over to the ticket window, with him right beside me.

"I just wanted to be sure you'd be home," he said. "We wouldn't want you to miss your own party."

"Party?" I said. "But John—"

He wouldn't even let me finish protesting.

"Now don't ask any questions, Lewis. You wouldn't want to spoil the surprise, would you?"

He chuckled. "Your plane's loading now. You'd better be going. Thanks for the ride, Lewis."

I went across to the plane and got in. I hoped that somehow we wouldn't have to spend that Martian anniversary being congratulated and petted and babied. I didn't think Martha could stand it. But there wasn't any polite way to say no.

*   *   *   *   *

It wasn't a long trip to the spaceport. In less than an hour the plane dropped down to the air strip that flanked the rocket field. But it was like flying from one civilization to another.

The city was big, almost like an Earth city. There was lots of traffic, cars and copters and planes. All the bustle of the spaceways stations.

But although the city looked like Earth, it smelled as dry and alkaline as all the rest of Mars.

I found the ticket office easily enough and went in. The young clerk barely glanced up at me. "Yes?" he said.

"I want to inquire about tickets to Earth," I said.

My hands were sweating, and I could feel my heart pounding too fast against my ribs. But my voice sounded casual, just the way I wanted it to sound.

"Tickets?" the clerk said. "How many?"

"Two. How much would they cost? Everything included."

"Forty-two eighty," he said. His voice was still bored. "I could give them to you for the flight after next. Tourist class, of course...."

We didn't have that much. We were at least three hundred short.

"Isn't there any way," I said hesitantly, "that I could get them for less? I mean, we wouldn't need insurance, would we?"

He looked up at me for the first time, startled. "You don't mean you want them for yourself, do you?"

"Why yes. For me and my wife."

He shook his head. "I'm sorry," he said flatly. "But that would be impossible in any case. You're too old."

He turned away from me and bent over his desk work again.

The words hung in the air. Too old ... too old ... I clutched the edge of the desk and steadied myself and forced down the panic I could feel rising.

"Do you mean," I said slowly, "that you wouldn't sell us tickets even if we had the money?"

He glanced up again, obviously annoyed at my persistence. "That's right. No passengers over seventy carried without special visas. Medical precaution."

I just stood there. This couldn't be happening. Not after all our years of working and saving and planning for the future. Not go back. Not even next year. Stay here, because we were old and frail and the ships wouldn't be bothered with us anyway.

Martha.... How could I tell her? How could I say, "We can't go home, Martha. They won't let us."

I couldn't say it. There had to be some other way.

"Pardon me," I said to the clerk, "but who should I see about getting a visa?"

He swept the stack of papers away with an impatient gesture and frowned up at me.

"Over at the colonial office, I suppose," he said. "But it won't do you any good."

I could read in his eyes what he thought of me. Of me and all the other farmers who lived in the outlying districts and raised crops and seldom came to the city. My clothes were old and provincial and out of style, and so was I, to him.

"I'll try it anyway," I said.

He started to say something, then bit it back and looked away from me again. I was keeping him from his work. I was just a rude old man interfering with the operation of the spaceways.

Slowly I let go of the desk and turned to leave. It was hard to walk. My knees were trembling, and my whole body shook. It was all I could do not to cry. It angered me, the quavering in my voice and the weakness in my legs.

I went out into the hall and looked for the directory that would point the way to the colonial office. It wasn't far off.

I walked out onto the edge of the field and past the Earth rocket, its silver nose pointed up at the sky. I couldn't bear to look at it for longer than a minute.

It was only a few hundred yards to the colonial office, but it seemed like miles.

*   *   *   *   *

This office was larger than the other, and much more comfortable. The man seated behind the desk seemed friendlier too.

"May I help you?" he asked.

"Yes," I said slowly. "The man at the ticket office told me to come here. I wanted to see about getting a permit to go back to Earth...."

His smile faded. "For yourself?"

"Yes," I said woodenly. "For myself and my wife."

"Well, Mr...."

"Farwell. Lewis Farwell."

"My name's Duane. Please sit down, won't you?... How old are you, Mr. Farwell?"

"Eighty-seven," I said. "In Earth years."

He frowned. "The regulations say no space travel for people past seventy, except in certain special cases...."

I looked down at my hands. They were shaking badly. I knew he could see them shake, and was judging me as old and weak and unable to stand the trip. He couldn't know why I was trembling.

"Please," I whispered. "It wouldn't matter if it hurt us. It's just that we want to see Earth again. It's been so long...."

"How long have you been here, Mr. Farwell?" It was merely politeness. There wasn't any promise in his voice.

"Sixty-five years." I looked up at him. "Isn't there some way—"

"Sixty-five years? But that means you must have come here on the first colonizing ship."

"Yes," I said. "We did."

"I can't believe it," he said slowly. "I can't believe I'm actually looking at one of the pioneers." He shook his head. "I didn't even know any of them were still on Mars."

"We're the last ones," I said. "That's the main reason we want to go back. It's awfully hard staying on when your friends are dead."

*   *   *   *   *

Duane got up and crossed the room to the window and looked out over the rocket field.

"But what good would it do to go back, Mr. Farwell?" he asked. "Earth has changed very much in the last sixty-five years."

He was trying to soften the disappointment. But nothing could. If only I could make him realize that.

"I know it's changed," I said. "But it's *home.* Don't you see? We're Earthmen still. I guess that never changes. And now that we're old, we're aliens here."

"We're all aliens here, Mr. Farwell."

"No," I said desperately. "Maybe you are. Maybe a lot of the city people are. But our neighbors were born on Mars. To them Earth is a legend. A place where their ancestors once lived. It's not real to them...."

He turned and crossed the room and came back to me. His smile was pitying. "If you went back," he said, "you'd find you were a Martian, too."

I couldn't reach him. He was friendly and pleasant and he was trying to make things easier, and it wasn't any use talking. I bent my head and choked back the sobs I could feel rising in my throat.

"You've lived a full life," Duane said. "You were one of the pioneers. I remember reading about your ship when I was a boy, and wishing I'd been born sooner so that I could have been on it."

Slowly I raised my head and looked up at him.

"Please," I said. "I know that. I'm glad we came here. If we had our lives to live over, we'd come again. We'd go through all the hardships of those first few years, and enjoy them just as much. We'd be just as thrilled over proving that it's possible to farm a world like this, where it's always freezing and the air is thin and nothing will grow outside the greenhouses. You don't need to tell me what we've done, or what we've gotten out of it. We know. We've had a wonderful life here."

"But you still want to go back?"

"Yes," I said. "We still want to go back. We're tired of living in the past, with our friends dead and nothing to do except remember."

He looked at me for a long moment. Then he said slowly, "You realize, don't you, that if you went back to Earth you'd have to stay there? You couldn't return to Mars...."

"I realize that," I said. "That's what we want. We want to die at home. On Earth."

*   *   *   *   *

For a long, long moment his eyes never left mine. Then, slowly, he sat down at his desk and reached for a pen.

"All right, Mr. Farwell," he said. "I'll give you a visa."

I couldn't believe it. I stared at him, sure that I'd misunderstood.

"Sixty-five years...." He shook his head. "I only hope I'm doing the right thing. I hope you won't regret this."

"We won't," I whispered.

Then I remembered that we were still short of money. That that was why I'd come to the spaceport originally. I was almost afraid to mention it, for fear I'd lose everything.

"Is there—is there some way we could be excused from the insurance?" I said. "So we could go back this year? We're three hundred short."

He smiled. It was a very reassuring smile. "You don't need to worry about the money," he said. "The colonial office can take care of that. After all, we owe your generation a great debt, Mr. Farwell. A passport tax and the fare to Earth are little enough to pay for a planet."

I didn't quite understand him, but that didn't matter. The only thing that mattered was that we were going home. Back to Earth. I could see Martha's face when I told her. I could see her tears of happiness....

There were tears on my own cheeks, but I wasn't ashamed of them now.

"Mr. Farwell," Duane said. "You go back home. The shuttle ship will be leaving in a few minutes."

"You mean that—" I started.

He nodded. "I'll get your tickets for you. On the first ship I can. Just leave it to me."

"It's too much trouble," I protested.

"No it's not." He smiled. "Besides, I'd like to bring them out to you. I'd like to see your farm, if I may."

Then I remembered what John Emery had said this morning about our anniversary. It would be a wonderful celebration, now that there was something to celebrate. We could even save our announcement that we were going home until then.

"Mr. Duane," I said. "Next week, on the tenth, we'll have been here thirty-five Martian years. Maybe you'd like to come out then. I guess our neighbors will be giving us a sort of party."

He laid the pen down and looked at me very intently. "They don't know you're planning to leave yet, do they?"

"No. We'll wait and tell them then."

Duane nodded slowly. "I'll be there," he promised.

*   *   *   *   *

Martha was out on the veranda again, looking down the road toward the village. All afternoon at least one of us had been out there watching for our guests, waiting for our anniversary celebration to begin.

"Do you see anyone yet?" I called.

"No," she said. "Not yet...."

I looked around the room hoping I'd find something left undone that I could work on, so I wouldn't have to sit and worry about the possibility of Duane's having forgotten us. But everything was ready. The extra chairs were out and the furniture all dusted, and Martha's cakes and cookies arranged on the table.

I couldn't sit still. Not today. I got up out of the chair and joined her on the veranda.

"I wonder what their surprise is...." she said. "Didn't John give you any hint at all?"

"No," I said. "But whatever it is, it can't be half as wonderful as ours."

She reached for my hand. "Lewis," she whispered. "I can hardly believe it, can you?"

"No," I said. "But it's true. We're really going."

I put my arm around her, and she rested her head against me.

"I'm so happy, Lewis."

Her cheeks were full of color once again, and her step had a spring to it that I hadn't seen for years. It was as if the years of waiting were falling away from both of us now.

"I wish they'd come," she said. "I can hardly wait to see their faces when we tell them."

It was getting late in the afternoon. Already the sun was dipping down toward the desert horizon. It was hard to wait. In some ways it was harder to be patient these last few hours than it had been during all those years we'd wanted to go back.

"Look," Martha said suddenly. "There's a car now."

Then I saw the car too, coming quickly toward us. It pulled up in front of the house and stopped and Duane stepped out.

"Well, hello there, Mr. Farwell," he called. "All ready for the trip?"

I nodded. Suddenly, now that he was here, I couldn't say anything at all.

He must have seen how excited we were. By the time he was inside the veranda door he'd reached into his wallet and pulled out a long envelope.

"Here's your schedule," he said. "Your tickets are all made out for next week's flight."

Martha's hand crept into mine. "You've been so kind," she whispered.

*   *   *   *   *

We went into the house and smiled at each other while Duane admired the furniture and the farming district in general and our place in particular. We hardly heard what he was saying.

When the doorbell rang we stared at each other. For a minute I couldn't think who it might be. I'd forgotten our guests and their surprise party, even the anniversary itself had slipped my mind.

"Hello in there," John Emery called. "Come on out, you two."

Martha pressed my hand once more. Then she stepped to the door and opened it.

"Happy anniversary!"

We stood frozen. We'd expected only a few visitors, some of our nearest neighbors. But the yard was full of people. They crowded up our walk and in the road and more of them were still piling out of cars. It looked as if everyone in the district was along.

"Come on out," Emery called. "You too, Duane."

The two men smiled at each other knowingly, and for just a moment I had time to wonder why.

Then Martha clutched my arm. "You tell him, Lewis."

"John," I said. "We have a surprise for you too—"

He wouldn't let me finish. He took hold of my arm with one hand and Martha's with the other and drew us outside where everyone could see us.

"You can tell us later, Lewis," he said, "First we have a surprise for you!"

"But wait—"

They crowded in around us, laughing and waving and calling "Happy anniversary". We couldn't resist them. They swept us along with them down the walk and into one of the cars.

I looked around for Duane. He was in the back seat, smiling somewhat nervously. Perhaps he thought that this was normal farm life.

"Lewis," Martha said, "where are they taking us?"

"I don't know...."

The cars started, ours leading the way. It was a regular procession back to the village, with everyone laughing and calling to us and telling us how happy we were going to be with our surprise. Every time we tried to ask questions, John Emery interrupted.

"Just wait and see," he kept saying. "Wait and see...."

*   *   *   *   *

At the end of the village square they'd put up a platform. It wasn't very big, nor very well made, but it was strung with yards of bunting and a huge sign that said, "Happy Anniversary, Lewis and Martha."

We were pushed toward it, carried along by the swarm of people. There wasn't any way to resist. Martha clung to my arm, pressing close against me. She was trembling again.

"What does it mean, Lewis?"

"I wish I knew."

They pushed us right up onto the platform and John Emery followed us up and held out his hand to quiet the crowd. I put my arm around Martha and looked down at them. Hundreds of people. All in their best clothes. Our friends's children and grandchildren, and even great-grandchildren.

"I won't make a speech," John Emery said when they were finally quiet. "You know why we're here today—all of you except Lewis and Martha know. It's an anniversary. A big anniversary. Thirty-five years today since our fathers—and you two—landed here on Mars...."

He paused. He didn't seem to know what to say next. Finally he turned and swept his arm past the platform to where a big canvas-covered object stood on the ground.

"Unveil it," he said.

The crowd grew absolutely quiet. A couple of boys stepped up and pulled the canvas off.

"There's your surprise," John Emery said softly.

It was a statue. A life-size statue carved from the dull red stone of Mars. Two figures, a man and a woman, dressed in farm clothes, standing side by side and looking out across the square toward the open desert.

They were very real, those figures. Real, and somehow familiar.

"Lewis," Martha whispered. "They're—they're us!"

She was right. It was a statue of us. Neither old nor young, but ageless. Two farmers, looking out forever across the endless Martian desert....

There was an inscription on the base, but I couldn't quite make it out. Martha could. She read it, slowly, while everyone in the crowd stood silent, listening.

"Lewis and Martha Farwell," she read. "The last of the pioneers—" Her voice broke. "Underneath," she whispered, "it says—the first Martians. And then it lists them—us...."

She read the list, all the names of our friends who had come out on that first ship. The names of men and women who had died, one by one, and left their farms to their children—to the same children who now crowded close about the platform and listened to her read, and smiled up at us.

She came to the end of the list and looked out at the crowd. "Thank you," she whispered.

They shouted then. They called out to us and pressed forward and held their babies up to see us.

*   *   *   *   *

I looked out past the people, across the flat red desert to the horizon, toward the spot in the east where the Earth would rise, much later. The dry smell of Mars had never been stronger.

The first Martians....

They were so real, those carved figures. Lewis and Martha Farwell....

"Look at them, Lewis," Martha said softly. "They're cheering us. Us!"

She was smiling. There were tears in her eyes, but her smile was bright and proud and shining. Slowly she turned away from me and straightened, staring out over the heads of the crowd across the desert to the east. She stood with her head thrown back and her mouth smiling, and she was as proudly erect as the statue that was her likeness.

"Martha," I whispered. "How can we tell them goodbye?"

Then she turned to face me, and I could see the tears glistening in her eyes. "We can't leave, Lewis. Not after this."

She was right, of course. We couldn't leave. We were symbols. The last of the pioneers. The first Martians. And they had carved their symbol in our image and made us a part of Mars forever.

I glanced down, along the rows of upturned, laughing faces, searching for Duane. He was easy to find. He was the only one who wasn't shouting. His eyes met mine, and I didn't have to say anything. He knew. He climbed up beside me on the platform.

I tried to speak, but I couldn't.

"Tell him, Lewis," Martha whispered. "Tell him we can't go."

Then she was crying. Her smile was gone and her proud look was gone and her hand crept into mine and trembled there. I put my arm around her shoulders, but there was no way I could comfort her.

"Now we'll never go," she sobbed. "We'll never get home...."

I don't think I had ever realized, until that moment, just how much it meant to her—getting home. Much more, perhaps, than it had ever meant to me.

The statues were only statues. They were carved from the stone of Mars. And Martha wanted Earth. We both wanted Earth. Home....

I looked away from her then, back to Duane. "No," I said. "We're still going. Only—" I broke off, hearing the shouting and the cheers and the children's laughter. "Only, how can we tell *them*?"

Duane smiled. "Don't try to, Mr. Farwell," he said softly. "Just wait and see."

He turned, nodded to where John Emery still stood at the edge of the platform. "All right, John."

Emery nodded too, and then he raised his hand. As he did so, the shouting stopped and the people stood suddenly quiet, still looking up at us.

"You all know that this is an anniversary," John Emery said. "And you all know something else that Lewis and Martha thought they'd kept as a surprise—that this is more than an anniversary. It's goodbye."

I stared at him. He knew. All of them knew. And then I looked at Duane and saw that he was smiling more than ever.

"They've lived here on Mars for thirty-five years," John Emery said. "And now they're going back to Earth."

Martha's hand tightened on mine. "Look, Lewis," she cried. "Look at them. They're not angry. They're—they're happy for us!"

John Emery turned to face us. "Surprised?" he said.

I nodded. Martha nodded too. Behind him, the people cheered again.

"I thought you would be," Emery said. Then, "I'm not very good at speeches, but I just wanted you to know how much we've enjoyed being your neighbors. Don't forget us when you get back to Earth."

*   *   *   *   *

It was a long, long trip from Mars to Earth. Three months on the ship, thirty-five million miles. A trip we had dreamed about for so long, without any real hope of ever making it. But now it was over. We were back on Earth. Back where we had started from.

"It's good to be alone, isn't it, Lewis?" Martha leaned back in her chair and smiled up at me.

I nodded. It did feel good to be here in the apartment, just the two of us, away from the crowds and the speeches and the official welcomes and the flashbulbs popping.

"I wish they wouldn't make such a fuss over us," she said. "I wish they'd leave us alone."

"You can't blame them," I said, although I couldn't help wishing the same thing. "We're celebrities. What was it that reporter said about us? That we're part of history...."

She sighed. She turned away from me and looked out the window again, past the buildings and the lighted traffic ramps and the throngs of people bustling by outside, people who couldn't see in through the one-way glass, people whom we couldn't hear because the room was soundproofed.

"Mars should be up by now," she said.

"It probably is." I looked out again, although I knew that we would see nothing. No stars. No planets. Not even the moon, except as a pale half disc peering through the haze. The lights from the city were too bright. The air held the light and reflected it down again, and the sky was a deep, dark blue with the buildings about us towering into it, outlined blackly against it. And we couldn't see the stars....

"Lewis," Martha said slowly. "I never thought it would have changed this much, did you?"

"No." I couldn't tell from her voice whether she liked the changes or not. Lately I couldn't tell much of anything from her voice. And nothing was the same as we had remembered it.

Even the Earth farms were mechanized now. Factory production lines for food, as well as for everything else. It was necessary, of course. We had heard all the reasons, all the theories, all the latest statistics.

"I guess I'll go to bed soon," Martha said. "I'm tired."

"It's the higher gravity." We'd both been tired since we got back to Earth. We had forgotten, over the years, what Earth gravity was like.

She hesitated. She smiled at me, but her eyes were worried. "Lewis—are you really glad we came back?"

It was the first time she had asked me that. And there was only one answer I could give her. The one she expected.

"Of course, Martha...."

She sighed again. She got up out of the chair and turned toward the bedroom door, and then she paused there by the window looking out at the deep blue sky.

"Are you really glad, Lewis?"

Then I knew. Or, at least, I hoped. "Why, Martha? Aren't you?"

For one long minute she stood beside me, looking up at the Mars we couldn't see. And then she turned to face me once again, and I could see the tears.

"Oh, Lewis, I want to go home!"

Full circle. We had both come full circle these last few hectic weeks on Earth.

"So do I, Martha."

"Do you, Lewis?" And then the tiredness came back to her eyes and she looked away again. "But of course we can't."

Slowly I crossed over to the desk and opened the top drawer and took out the folder that Duane had given me, that last day at the spaceport, just before our ship to Earth had blasted off. Slowly I unfolded the paper that Duane had told me to keep in case we ever wanted it.

"Yes, we can, Martha. We can go back."

"What's that, Lewis?" And then she saw what it was. Her face came alive again, and her eyes were shining. "We're going home?" she whispered. "We're really going home?"

I looked down at the Earth-Mars half of the round trip ticket that Duane had given me, and I knew that this time she was right.

This time we'd really be going home.

And Now a Message . . .
By Greg Fowlkes

A short Story from the upcoming Book - *Back Road to the Stars*

© 2010 Greg Fowlkes

AND NOW A MESSAGE . . .

For the third time that night Jack Olsen was about to nod off over the copy of *Statistical Information Theory* that he was attempting to read. Giving it up as a bad effort, he shut the book and looked out the window of the control room at the giant bowl of the Arecibo radio telescope. Theoretically he was running the huge instrument, but in reality all the controlling was being done by the computers in the room around him. For six months he had been working eight hour shifts every night, and his job had consisted of the five minutes a shift that it took to enter the coordinates to be examined on the control console. Other than that, he was on hand only for the off chance that the monitoring programs would recognize some pattern in the radio noise, in which case an alarm would sound. So far, in the six months, it hadn't happened.

He walked over to the coffee machine in the hopes that a cup would revive him enough so that he could continue his studies. He never made it, for as if to prove the lie of his earlier thoughts, the alarm sounded. For a moment Jack was frozen, the alarm beating raucously in his ears, then he pulled himself together and flicked off the switch on the bell. With the room returned to the relative quiet of the whoosh of the cooling fans on the equipment, Jack sat down at the console and keyed in an enquiry. Within seconds the computer had replied that it was receiving a strong periodic signal on the 42 centimeter band. Further questioning showed that it was not a program malfunction but a genuine signal.

Jack picked up the phone and dialed his boss's number. It was three in the morning, but his instructions had been clear. If anything was received that could possibly be an intelligent signal, he was supposed to contact his superior immediately.

Despite the long drive through the mountains in the cool Puerto Rican night, Professor Kraft showed up with his eyes still sleepy. Shuffling over to the coffee pot by the window he poured himself a large mug before he said anything. "You'd better have something good to get me up at this hour."

"I think so," Jack said, aware that his boss's irritation was only feigned. "I've been checking with the computer since I called you. It shows a strong periodic signal with a sharp pulse every fifty milliseconds. It runs on like that for about two and a half minutes before the signal fades below the background."

"Any chance that it might be a pulsar?" Kraft asked, referring to the radio signals of rapidly rotating neutron stars. "That's within the range of periods for them. When the first one was discovered, they thought that they had received intelligent signals."

"I thought of that, so I checked the record of the broad band receiver." Jack brought out a long strip of graph paper and pointed to the evenly spaced patterns of peaks on it. "Where the narrow band shows only a single repetitive pulse, the wide band gives us this fine structure. It's far too regular to be a pulsar and much too detailed. It's more like some sort of timing signal or spacer. And in between the pulses there is another signal. It's not as repetitive as the main pulse. That's why the program doesn't bring it out. But there definitely is some sort of transmission in between. It's weaker, but I think that we can write a processing program to pick it out from the noise."

Kraft looked at the trace in his hand thoughtfully. "I hate to make snap judgements. You can be suckered in too easily that way. But it does look like some kind of artificial signal. We'll get the team working on it in the morning. Have you received any additional signals?"

"No. I've kept the dish tracking the source, but all we get on 42 cm. is background noise. It's like there was a moment of freak atmospheric conditions that opened a window, and then it shut again. Just like you get with shortwave sometimes because of the ionosphere."

"Well, we should be grateful for what we've got. I don't think I can sleep anymore tonight, so I'll keep you company. I'd like to be here if we get any more messages from our friends out there," he said, pointing with his cup towards the star filled sky that loomed over the radio telescope's antenna.

"Frustrating, isn't it?" Prof. Kraft remarked to the team of graduate students and post doctoral fellows that were working under him on the interstellar communications project. And frustrating it had been. For six months they had continuously monitored the sky searching for signs of life finally to be rewarded by a two minute snippet of extraterrestrial conversation.

Now, another six months later, they had still made no sense of the signal, nor had they received any further transmissions from that part of the sky, though they had concentrated their efforts in that direction.

"Rumors have leaked out about our discovery, and I've been getting requests for the data. I'd sure hate to have someone else steal our thunder by deciphering the signal, but if we don't make some progress soon, we're going to have to release it." He looked around the table at the young faces of his assistants. At the moment they didn't look nearly as bright and intelligent as he knew they were.

"Why don't I summarize what we've found so far in hopes that it will give us some new ideas?"

"First, we've got this repetitive pattern of pulses every twentieth of a second as regular as clockwork. So regular, in fact, that we can't decide whether they serve as breaks in the message or were just put there to attract our attention. Remember, it was these pulses that were first recognized by the computer."

"But the pulses aren't the real message. That lays in the spaces in between. We've been able to deduce that the messages are digitized and the computer has been able to enhance them so that we have a fairly error free record of them. There is some repetitive structure to them, and they do vary in some sort of progression, but beyond that, we haven't been able to get the least notion of what they mean. Anyone have something to add?"

Bill Warden, one of the post docs, spoke up. "Well, we've tried mathematical analysis on the signals and have gotten zero results. It has already been assumed that any sort of interstellar communications would be based on sort of easily recognizable mathematical progression. Like one, two three. Something like that to show that they were rational. From there you can always build up more complicated concepts."

"With this message we don't have that, which leads us to one of two assumptions. One, we have only a fragment of a broadcast, and from a very advanced lesson at that. If that's the case, I don't see much hope of our being able to decipher the message until we can receive more signals to give us a broader base to work from."

"The other alternative is that they, whoever they are, just don't think like us. Their minds work in some fashion so that this mess we have makes sense to them. If so, I don't see any hope at all. Their minds may just be too foreign for us to hold a dialog with them."

"Thank you for that optimistic note," Prof. Kraft said wryly. "For the first time mankind has received a message from another species and we can't tell whether it is a cure for cancer, a means of achieving universal peace, or a recipe for sauerbratten. Any comments?"

"If it's sauerbratten, where do we go for a tablespoon of powdered bandersnatch egg?" quipped one of the grad students. They all laughed at the joke more than it deserved. Six months of unrewarded work had left them all a little giddy. After the giggles and comments had died down, Jack Olsen coughed, trying to get their attention.

"You've got something useful to say, Jack?" Kraft asked. "You might as well tell us. I don't think anyone else has anything useful to add," he said, pointedly looking at the wisecracker.

"I've been thinking about the signal, and I remember something that I said to you the night it came in. I don't know if you recall, but I called the pulses timing signals. Now there is one type of common transmission that has the same kind of pulses, and that's television. They use the pulses to synchronize the frames. It's possible that the message in between each pulse is a picture, and the whole transmission is meant to be viewed in sequence."

"How long have you been sitting on this while the rest of us were beating our brains out?" Kraft asked.

"It just came to me," Jack said, his face flushed. "I should have thought of it earlier, but like Bill said, we've all been conditioned to look for something like one plus one equals two."

"I think that we should all have seen it," Kraft said. "It makes as much sense as anything else that's been suggested. Do you think that you can get us a picture?"

"If it's there, I should be able to pick it out using the computer," Jack answered.

"Good. Then, since it was your idea, you're in charge. Dragoon anything or anybody that you need to help you."

Five days later they were all gathered around the conference room table again, but this time there was a TV set and a video recorder on a cart at its end. From the nervous stubbing of cigarette butts and fingers drumming on the table, it was obvious that all the members of the team were in a state of anticipation.

"It took some time to figure out exactly how the signal was put together," Jack began. "After all, we didn't know how many lines there were in each frame or how many bits made up each unit of picture. In the end, I had to have the computer run through all the likely possibilities for one of the frames. It took a lot of computer time, but I've finally got some recognizable pictures."

"It turns out that the original broadcast was in color. That threw us for a while, but we finally psyched it out. The aliens must have eyes structurally different from ours; there are only two colors, not three in the signal. Which colors they are is anybody's guess. They might be ultraviolet and infrared for all we can tell. Arbitrarily, I've assigned them red and bluish green, so keep that in mind. Also, because the video recorder uses thirty frames a second instead of the twenty in the transmission, it was necessary to compress the program a bit. This means that everything you'll be seeing has been speeded up about fifty percent.

"I guess you're all more interested in seeing the tape than in listening to me." A snort from Prof. Kraft indicated agreement. Jack flicked off the lights and started the tape. For a minute the screen showed only snow, then a face became recognizable. It was a sickly chartreuse, and there was no nose between the two large, oval eyes, but it was recognizable as a face. The figures movements were quick and jerky like an old silent movie, the result of the difference in frame speed, and the picture left a lot to be desired in clarity, the product of interstellar noise, but it was a picture, the first of an alien race.

As the tape played, a weird, sings song voice came from the speaker sounding something like a Chinese chipmunk. "I forgot to mention that there was also an audio track along with the signal. Again, it's only a reconstruction and may not bear much resemblance to the original, but then, we'll never know," Jack commented. They had determined that the source of the transmission was at least several dozen light years away. It would take twice that number of years to send a message and receive a reply, by which time they would all be dead.

They continued to watch the tape. The camera had drawn back to show the alien from the waist up revealing rounded shoulders and a pair of six fingered hands. Apparently he was standing behind a low lectern or a table of some sort. The fuzzy picture and camera angle made it hard to tell which. As he, or her, or it, spoke, the alien pointed at a chart or poster suspended on the backdrop. A pattern of red and blue that hurt the eye with violent contrasts seemed to be some sort of text. The voice continued as the picture disappeared in a sea of snow and then it broke into static. The transmission had ended.

"You've done a fine job, Jack," Prof. Kraft said after they had played the tape through a half dozen times. "It's actually far better than I thought it would be, and I think we can accept any of the shortcomings that you mentioned."

"So, we've got a face and body of what certainly is a rational creature. He seemed to be giving us a lesson or lecture of some sort, though I for one don't have the faintest idea of what he was talking about. We have an idea of what they look like which I am sure will give the biologists a lot to speculate on, so I guess that we should be thankful for small favors, but I still don't see how we're going to learn any more about them without receiving further signals."

"I wouldn't hold out much hope of that," Jack interjected. "I think that it's clear now that the signal we picked up was not meant for interstellar communication. Any such signal would have been designed with much greater noise immunity. We were able to receive it only because of an accident of atmospheric conditions. It was actually just a local TV broadcast. As we haven't received anything since, those conditions must be rare."

"So," Kraft said, "we have a message of great potential import, that at the very least could provide us with insights on a totally alien culture, and no way to decipher it."

"I've got an idea," Bill said. "We've all been looking at the problem from the point of view of hardware and computer programs. That's natural because of our backgrounds, but now that we have what amounts to an artifact, maybe we should call in a specialist. We need someone who is trained in resurrecting a culture from its fragments. I suggest that we show the tape to some archeologists and get their opinions."

Convincing an archeologist to look at the tape was harder than it had sounded. Most of them were more interested in ancient rather than alien civilizations. Jack suspected that they felt out of their depth with the computers and electronics. With some pressure and pleading, a group finally agreed to view the tape, but after the showing, only one evinced any interest in following up on it.

A visiting lecturer from Norway, she was reputed to have a good background in languages, though Jack lacked the knowledge to judge her qualifications. However, as she was young, blond, and attractive, he was quite willing to spend the time required to familiarize her with the tape and the equipment they had used to come up with it. Together, they spent hours viewing the tape, studying it frame by frame attempting to pick out the slightest piece of information.

The project team had been assembled in the conference room, and this time it was the archeologist's turn to address them. For three weeks Cristina Peterson had been studying the tape almost constantly, and now she was ready to give her opinion. With the exception of Jack, who had been working closely with her, they were all, even Prof. Kraft, eagerly awaiting the report. There had been a great deal of speculation about what her findings would be.

"First," she began, "before I get your hopes up, I want to say that I have not been able to get a word for word translation of the voice on the tape. The sample of speech is just too brief for that to be possible. If the scene had contained more action, I might have been more successful, but we were not that fortunate. I have, however, been able to form a hypothesis based on the spoken word as well as visual clues such as facial expression, setting, and so on."

"An important point to remember is that the aliens, despite certain differences in appearance, are not too dissimilar from ourselves. They are bipedal, intelligent, and possess opposable thumbs. They have binocular vision and a form of color perception as well. Brain size is about the same in relationship to total body size as in humans, and I would be greatly surprised if they were much larger or smaller than ourselves. That much can be guessed on the basis of physiology from the picture and the nature of the signal. From this information, I think that we can draw the conclusion that their planet is, within limits, earthlike."

"Probably more relevant is their state of culture. They obviously have a technology and one that is recognizable in terms of our own. That we can receive their signals is proof of that. Also, they speak, they wear clothing, we can even guess at the purpose of some of the objects visible in the tape. I might add that this is more than we can do for some of the artifacts of primitive human cultures. In some ways we have more in common with the aliens than we do with the Tasadi or Bushman."

"I want you to bear in mind that these beings are not greatly different from ourselves. If we are to properly analyze the contents of the message, we must remember that they are influenced by the same drives and forces as humans." There was an uneasy shifting in their seats on the part of the team members as they took in the meaning of her statement.

"If we accept this premise, and replace the alien with a human, we can make an educated guess as to what we are seen on the tape. I'll run it again for you so that you can make the substitution." Jack tapped the switch, and for the next minute and a half they watched the now familiar scene replay itself.

"Before I give my own opinion, would anyone else like to make a guess?" Cristina asked.

Kraft looked around the room, but it appeared as though no one had the courage to be the first to put his own views forward. To break the silence he said, "It's only a guess, but to start the discussion, I'd say that the alien might be a lecturer. He's obviously standing at some sort of podium or speaker's table."

"He seems a little too impassioned for a lecturer, at least in the physical sciences," one of the grad students remarked. "I've never seen you that excited before a class." Kraft smiled at the reference to his own low keyed classroom delivery.

"Maybe it's a political science class. They get more aroused."

Bill Warden broke in, "Why a class? It looks to me more like he's a politician trying to persuade the voters. He must be up for reelection. The sign in back could be an election poster." That brought a couple of laughs and a few less than serious comments.

"We've all had a crack at it," Prof. Kraft said. "You obviously have your own interpretation, and I think that we've been kept in suspense long enough. From the look on Jack's face, it must be a good one. Let's hear it now. After all, the communication between two species is one of the most important events in human history."

She smiled at the jibe. "All your suggestions are plausible, but I've spent more time analyzing the tape than you have. I'll play it again for you and point out the features that have led me to my interpretation."

"The first thing that caught my attention was the fact that the word 'gratach' was mentioned fourteen times, an unusually high incidence in such a brief speech. Furthermore, at least four of those times the speaker pointed to the symbols on the chart behind him. I think that we can assume that 'gratach' is a name, and the symbols form the written version."

"Now here's something that I want you to see." She froze the picture on the television. "Note the artifacts on the table, a bowl filled with a substance and a box or container. There appears to be some writing on the box, but the resolution of the picture isn't good enough to allow us to make it out. However," she said as the tape began to roll again, "as the alien points to the box and says 'gratach' it is likely that the symbols again spell out the name in the chart behind the alien. Note, too, the expression on his face. Despite the lack of a nose, the face is surprisingly human, and if that expression was on a human face, it would be one of approval or pleasure."

"I think that if you put all the clues together, you can come to only one conclusion. Dr. Warden was not far off when he suggested a political campaign. The speaker is definitely trying to persuade his audience, but it is the package, not himself, that he is trying to sell."

"Oh, god," Kraft sputtered. "You can't mean it. The first communication from another planet and it's only . . ."

"Yes, I'm afraid so," Cristina said. "The first and only signal received from another world is nothing more than a breakfast food commercial."

Also From Resurrected Press
SCIENCE FICTION AUTHORS RESURRECTED

FYFE RESURRECTED - THE STORIES OF H. B. FYFE

Stories from the Golden Age of Science Fiction by the author of D-99. dealing with the interaction of humans and aliens on far off worlds in ways that were as creative as they were imaginative.

SCHMITZ RESURRECTED - SELECTED STORIES OF JAMES H. SCHMITZ

Includes "An Incident on Route 12", "Watch the Sky", "The Other Likeness", "The Star Hyacinths", "Oneness", "The Winds of Time", "Ham Sandwich" and "Gone Fishing".

SHECKLY RESURRECTED - THE EARLY STORIES OF ROBERT SHECKLEY

Resurrected Press has collected some of the best of these from the 50's including "Warrior Race", "The Leech", "Watchbird", "Warm", "Diplomatic Immunity", "The Hour of Battle", "Besides Still Waters", "Keep Your Shape", "One Man's Poison", 'Ask a Foolish Question", "Cost of Living", "Death Wish Forever".

DICK RESURRECTED - THE EARLY STORIES OF PHILIP K. DICK

Early stories from the author of the novels that inspired "Blade Runner," "Total Recall," and "A Scanner Darkly".

HAMILTON RESURRECTED - CLASSIC STORIES OF EDMOND HAMILTON

Edmond Hamilton was one of the most popular writers during the 30's and 40's, the period that saw the first flowering of modern science fiction.

SMITH RESURRECTED - SELECTED STORIES OF EVELYN E. SMITH

During an era when women rarely appeared in science fiction magazines, Evelyn E. Smith appeared regularly in the pages of Galaxy and Fantastic Universe. Resurrected Press is proud to return these stories to print.

NOURSE RESURRECTED - THE WORKS OF ALAN E. NOURSE

Alan E. Nourse was both a physician and a writer. He produced most of his work in that period known as the "Golden Age of Science Fiction. Best known for his novel Star Surgeon, he was also a prolific author of short stories during the 50's. This collection includes some of his best from that era including "Derelict," "The Coffin Cure," "Bear Trap," "Contamination Crew" and more.

LEINSTER RESURRECTED - SCIENCE FICTION STORIES FROM THE 1950's

For over five decades, Murray Leinster was one of the most respected names in science fiction. Though he began writing at the dawn of the pulp era his work evolved with the times. The ten stories collected here appeared during the 50's, that "Golden Age" of the genre. Spanning the gamut from alien invasions to alternate realities, they form a fitting display of his talents in what was his fourth decade as a writer.

OTHER CLASSIC SCIENCE FICTION NOVELS FROM RESURRECTED PRESS

TALENTS, INCORPORATED - BY MURRAY LEINSTER
When a Mekinese fleet conquers his home planet, Captain Bors turns to Talents, Incorporated for help using their collection of individuals with unusual abilities to defeat the enemy and save the galaxy.

THE PIRATES OF ERSATZ - BY MURRAY LEINSTER
Bran Hodden just wanted to be an electronic engineer and marry a delightful girl. But when he's framed by the powers on Walden he's forced to turn back to his family's trade, piracy. Also published as The Pirates of Zan.

EMPIRE - BY CLIFFORD SIMAK
Spencer Chambers and Interplanetary Power owned the Solar System because they controlled the source of power. It fell to Russell Page and Harry Wilson to challenge that control if they had to cross the universe to do it.

NIGHT OF THE LONG KNIVES - THE CREATURE FROM THE CLEVELAND DEPTHS - BY FRITZ LEIBER
Two classic novellas set in the not too distant future from a classic master of science fiction.

POLICE YOUR PLANET - BY LESTER DEL RAY
Of all the cities on all the planets of the Solar System, Marsport was the most corrupt. So when one-time prize-fighter, cop, and reporter, Bruce Gordon ends up with a one way ticket to Mars, it was only natural that he would find himself walking a beat collecting graft like the rest of the force. Just trying to survive, he finds himself caught in the middle between two rival gangs as they battle for control of the planet.

The Fictional Detective
by Greg Fowlkes

Who killed Ezekial O. Handler?

A beautiful dame, a hard-boiled private eye – and a dead body.

It started like any other case. When a famous writer dies in a mysterious car crash, private detective Frank Slade is called in to find answers, but all he finds is more questions. Who killed Ezekial Handler? Who is Janet Nielsen and why is she so interested in finding out? Who is leaving the neatly typed clues? And as Slade tries to find answers to these questions he starts to wonder if the ultimate answer will threaten his very existence.

Read about it in
The Fictional Detective

Visit www.thefictionaldetective.com

About Resurrected Press

A division of Intrepid Ink, LLC, Resurrected Press is dedicated to bringing high quality, vintage books back into publication. See our entire catalogue and find out more at www.ResurrectedPress.com.

About Intrepid Ink, LLC

Intrepid Ink, LLC provides full publishing services to authors of fiction and non-fiction books, eBooks and websites. From editing to formatting, from publishing to marketing, Intrepid Ink gets your creative works into the hands of the people who want to read them. Find out more at www.IntrepidInk.com.

www.ingramcontent.com/pod-product-compliance
Lightning Source LLC
Chambersburg PA
CBHW070003260626
47159CB00005B/1650